"Do you ever take a risk?"

Fiona's eyes widened as Wyatt stepped away from the doorjamb to close the distance between them. "What do you mean?"

"Do you ever drive over the speed limit? Accept a drink from a stranger?"

She shook her head so vehemently a strand of red hair slipped free of its tight knot.

"You don't know what you're missing..." He wanted to show her. He leaned a little closer—close enough to brush his mouth across hers.

Her breath shuddered out, warm and silky against his lips. And her thick lashes drifted down as her eyes closed. He deepened the kiss—as much as he could with a desk between them. He wanted to kick it aside, wanted nothing between his body and hers. He groaned at the thought.

And she jerked back as if she'd just awakened. Her chair creaked as it rolled her away from the desk— away from him. "I asked to meet with you just to talk," she said.

He uttered a sigh of disappointment. "That's too bad..."

Dear Reader,

While I have written for other Harlequin series, I've always been a fan of Blaze. So I'm thrilled to be writing my own Harlequin Blaze miniseries. Hotshots are the ultimate fire-fighting heroes. They're the men and women on the front line, battling the blaze. The heroes of Hotshot Heroes are brave and strong and sexy as hell. How is a heroine to resist them?

Cautious insurance agent Fiona O'Brien does her best, but she can't deny her red-hot attraction to Hotshot Wyatt Andrews. She resists her feelings, though, because she knows his profession is too dangerous. She won't risk her heart on a man like him. She saw how devastated her mother was when her father and stepfather both lost their lives because of the chances they'd taken.

So no matter how attracted she is to Wyatt, she doesn't intend to fall for him. But then a wildfire hits their town of Northern Lakes, Michigan, and she worries that it may be too late for her heart. Is it too late for Wyatt, too?

I hope you enjoy the exciting romance of Fiona and Wyatt!

Happy reading!

Lisa Childs

Lisa Childs

Red Hot

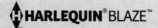

Recycling programs
for this product may
not exist in your area.

ISBN-13: 978-0-373-79880-3

Red Hot

Printed in U.S.A.

Ever since **Lisa Childs** read her first romance novel (a Harlequin story, of course) at age eleven, all she ever wanted was to be a romance writer. With over forty novels published with Harlequin, Lisa is living her dream. She is an award-winning, bestselling romance author. Lisa loves to hear from readers, who can contact her on Facebook, through her website, lisachilds.com, or her snail-mail address, PO Box 139, Marne, MI 49435.

Books by Lisa Childs

Harlequin Romantic Suspense

Bachelor Bodyguards

His Christmas Assignment

Harlequin Intrigue

Special Agents at the Altar

The Pregnant Witness
Agent Undercover
The Agent's Redemption

Shotgun Weddings

Groom Under Fire
Explosive Engagement
Bridegroom Bodyguard

Harlequin Nocturne

Taming the Shifter
Mistress of the Underworld

Witch Hunt

Haunted
Persecuted
Damned
Cursed

To get the inside scoop on Harlequin Blaze and its talented writers, be sure to check out BlazeAuthors.com.

All backlist available in ebook format.

Visit the Author Profile page at Harlequin.com for more titles.

To Andrew Ahearne—thank you for sharing your knowledge and past experience of the Forest Service Hotshots. Thank you, also, for making me believe that heroes are real!

1

"ARE YOU GOING to a fire?" the receptionist asked as Fiona O'Brien hurried past her desk in the blue and beige lobby of The Northern Lakes Insurance Agency.

Her briefcase swinging from her hand, she spun on a heel to turn back to Rita. "No, no fire…"

But her pulse was racing as if there was one. She drew in a deep breath and forced herself to calm down. Unfortunately, the old adage about redheads had proven true in her case, no matter how hard she tried to control her temper.

"I am going to see a firefighter, though," she admitted.

Rita arched a blond brow. "I would hope you're seeing him for a date, but since your weekly delivery of insipid carnations came today, I know you're still seeing the boring accountant."

Fiona cursed. She'd forgotten her date with Howard—although she wasn't certain how when they went to the same place on the same night at the same time every week. Actually, she did know how…

That damn firefighter.

"So do you have a *business* appointment with the firefighter?" Rita asked.

No. Wyatt Andrews had no idea she was coming to see him. Until the call she'd just taken, Fiona had had no idea and no desire to see Wyatt Andrews again, let alone talk to him. Not that she'd seen very much of him…

Six feet plus a few inches or more of muscle and arrogance and attitude. Black hair that was too long—like the stares from his brilliant blue eyes. Fortunately, she hadn't seen him that often over the past four or five years.

Nor had she ever really talked to him.

"So it's not business?" Rita prodded her.

Fiona shook her head and glared at the lock of hair that wriggled out of her bun to fall across her eyes. "There's no way I would ever sell a life insurance policy to a firefighter. The risk is too great."

Rita moved her thin shoulders in a shrug and casually remarked, "Everybody's going to die someday."

With her dyed blond hair and heavy makeup, the receptionist's age was impossible to determine. So Fiona didn't know if the other woman was too young or too old to care about death.

"But firefighting is a hazardous profession," Fiona said. "According to the statistics, a firefighter is far more likely to die than say…an accountant." And that was why she hadn't ever really talked to Wyatt Andrews on the few occasions she'd seen him. She had learned to not waste her time or her attention on a man with a death wish.

"If you marry ol' Howard, you might wish accountants died sooner," Rita warned her, her pale blue eyes glinting with laughter. "He might bore *you* to death."

Fiona would rather be bored than scared to death. And what her younger brother had told her moments earlier on the phone had scared her to death—or at least to outrage. She wasn't mad at *him*, though. She knew who'd put that outrageous, dangerous idea in his head: Wyatt Andrews.

Since he had become her brother's mentor six years ago, he'd had too much influence on Matthew's life. Now he was even endangering Matthew's life, or at the very least his future.

That was why she had to see Wyatt Andrews again. Why she had to have a real conversation with him. Her temper reignited, and she spun back toward the door.

But before Fiona could get away, Rita asked another question. "So if you're not going to date him and you're not going to sell him an insurance policy, why do you have to see this fireman?"

"To tell him to mind his own damn business!"

"Anybody ever tell you to mind your own damn business?"

Wyatt Andrews chuckled. Then he raised his hands, palms up, from the weights he'd been lifting. "Hey, it was just a suggestion!"

"That I need to get laid?"

Wyatt laughed harder at the outrage in his friend's deep voice. Captain Braden Zimmer glared at him from across the firehouse workout room. It was all white-washed cement block, no mirrors, no fancy mats. It was a serious room—because they had to be in serious shape. Their lives depended on it.

"You're the one who admitted you're all tense and edgy," Wyatt reminded him.

A muscle twitched along Braden's jaw, and he ran a hand over his brush-cut brown hair. It was still wet from his shower; he'd just finished working out when Wyatt had hit the gym. "Yeah, that's the way I get when there's a fire out there."

"But there isn't a fire." At least not one big enough for the forest service's elite unit of firefighters to have been called. Wildfire season hadn't even officially started yet. So the Huron Hotshots twenty-member team wasn't together yet. Just the firefighters who worked the off-season out of the Northern Lakes firehouse— he, Braden and a couple of other guys.

Braden glanced at the cell phone he clutched in one hand—probably checking for a missed call.

"The alarm would have gone off," Wyatt pointed out.

"I sent Dawson out to check for smoldering campsites."

"It's too early for camping. Too cold at night…" He shivered at the thought.

"There are some die-hard campers," Braden reminded him. "And they're the ones who build the biggest fires."

"If there was a big fire, Dawson would have called," he pointed out.

Braden shrugged. "Maybe the fire's just getting started…"

"Maybe you need something else to focus on besides your job," Wyatt suggested. "Like a woman…"

Braden glared at him again. "That's the last thing

I need. And who the hell are you to talk? I don't see you in a relationship."

Wyatt shuddered. "God, no."

A relationship was the last thing he wanted. Every guy he'd worked with who had settled down with a wife and kids had eventually left the job. Or in Braden's case, the wife had left him.

"That's the whole point, Captain," he told Braden. During the off-season, Braden was the captain of the Northern Lakes Fire Department. During the wildfire season, the retired captain resumed his position in Northern Lakes with a team of new forest service firefighter recruits, and Braden became superintendent of the Huron Hotshots team. In both positions, Wyatt was his assistant—one of two for the Hotshots and the only assistant for Northern Lakes. He was his professional wingman. Maybe it was time to make that personal, too. "You just got divorced. You don't want a relationship. You just want to have some fun."

"Fun?" Braden snorted with derision.

"You must've been married too long if you don't think sex is fun anymore." Another reason Wyatt never intended to get serious with anyone. Serious equaled boring.

Braden gave him another look. It wasn't a glare. It was more a pitying glance. Then he shook his head.

"What?" Wyatt asked. Nobody had ever pitied him before. Envied? Hell, yeah. Pitied? Never.

"You have no idea what you're talking about," Braden told him.

And nobody had ever accused Wyatt of not knowing women. "I don't know what the hell *you're* talking about." And he truly had no idea.

"Random sexual encounters don't sound fun," Braden explained. "They sound sad and empty."

Wyatt laughed, but it echoed oddly in the weight room, sounding hollow and uncertain. It wasn't as if Braden was getting to him. It wasn't as if Wyatt was about to question the lifestyle he'd chosen. He shook off those niggling doubts and laughed harder.

"You've been out of the game too long," Wyatt said. "You've forgotten what it's like to be single."

"Unfortunately I haven't…" Braden sighed. "I'm going to my office to make some calls. See if there's anything out there…"

He knew the captain was talking about fires. But he chose to be obtuse. "I'll show you what's out there," he offered. "I'm going to finish a few more reps before I hit the showers. Then I'll take you out on the town." Not that the village of Northern Lakes was much of a town. It was a resort area, though, and quite the party town during tourist season. "And I'll show you what you've been missing."

Braden laughed now. "You're the one who has no idea what you've been missing." His laughter continued, growing fainter as he walked out of the weight room.

Wyatt didn't get guys like Braden. The captain should have known better than anyone that the job and marriage didn't mix. And now that it was over, Braden needed to just move on instead of dwelling on it. Wyatt had never had any problem walking away after spending some time with a woman. But he'd been careful to date the right kind of woman—the kind who only wanted a good time, too. He steered clear—very clear—of women who wanted commitment. Because commitments led to marriage and ultimatums and heartbreak.

He shuddered again. Then he focused on the weights, lifting with renewed energy. Braden wasn't the only one who was feeling edgy. But at least Wyatt knew why he was. He'd been having some trouble finding those fun-loving girls. Of course, it wasn't tourist season yet.

It had been a long winter with spring just breaking through now. But it was a dry spring, which was conducive to fires—especially west of where they were based in northeastern Michigan. The Hotshots traveled the US and Canada, dropping in where they were needed to fight fires. Just as there was a tourist season in Northern Lakes, there was also a fire season. Usually the first fires started out west, where it was driest.

Maybe Braden was right.

Maybe there was something out there, just getting started.

Over his grunts, he caught the sound of footsteps against the cement floor of the weight room. Maybe Braden had realized *he* was right.

"Sheesh," he remarked without stopping his reps, "you must be super tense and edgy. You can't even wait until I'm finished, you want to get laid so badly."

He waited for Braden's laugh. No matter how glum the guy had been since his wife had left him, that was no excuse for losing his sense of humor. And Wyatt was damn funny. He even uttered a laugh at his own joke.

But it echoed off the cement walls with that same weird hollow sound. While he had only been razzing his friend to get him out of the funk Braden had been in since his divorce, Wyatt knew his joke had fallen flat. He settled the bar onto the bench rest and sat up, ready to be serious. He was a good listener—which he'd proven to Braden plenty when the captain's marital problems had begun.

He was also a good adviser when he wasn't being a smart-ass. He had a bachelor's degree in psychology and plenty of experience as a mentor for the county's youth services division. "I'm—" He swallowed the apology he'd been about to make and nearly swallowed his tongue, as well.

Braden wasn't the one who'd walked into the weight room. This person's green-eyed glare was far more lethal than the captain's. Fiona O'Brien stood before him—all fiery red hair and outrage.

"What the hell did you just say to me?" she demanded, her voice raspy with indignation.

He could have explained. He should have, really.

But on the few occasions he had seen Fiona O'Brien over the years, he'd never seen her like this. Oh, she'd glared at him before, but with more benign disdain— like a cat staring down at the puppy pissing on the carpet. Now her face was so flushed her freckles had disappeared into her complexion. And her body— which she insisted on concealing with businesslike suits—trembled with her temper. She'd always acted so cold and snobby around him that he hadn't thought she was capable of such passion. And he'd considered her good looks wasted on an empty, emotionless shell.

He'd had no idea what she'd been hiding beneath that flawless, impervious surface…

"What did I say?" He paraphrased her question as he jumped up from the weight bench and closed the distance between them. She stepped back, stumbling slightly on her high heels.

She might have only been wearing the heels because she was petite and wanted the extra height. Or maybe she wore them because they made her legs look longer, toned and sexy as hell. The beige suit couldn't hide her curves, either—not when the skirt was snug and ended above her knees.

Her eyes widened briefly in surprise at his nearness, but then narrowed in another glare. "You know what you said."

"That you must be really tense and edgy," he repeated the words he'd meant for his boss.

He should have pointed out that he'd had no way of knowing she was the one who'd walked into the weight room. He couldn't imagine why she had stopped by the firehouse at all. She had never gone out of her way to speak to him those few times they'd previously met. So why had she driven across town to seek him out now?

He wanted to know that. But he couldn't resist seeing just how much passion lurked beneath that beautiful surface. So he stepped closer to her as he said the rest, as if he meant the words for her, "You can't even wait until I'm finished, you want to get laid so badly."

His head snapped back as her hand connected—hard—with his face. His skin stung from the force of her slap. While she was petite, she packed a wallop. That wasn't quite the way he'd wanted to test her passion. So he jerked her up against him and lowered his head.

2

FIONA LIFTED HER hand to slap him again. But he caught her wrist and jerked her more tightly against him. The heat and dampness of his sweat-slick bare chest penetrated her suit jacket and blouse, burning her skin.

Or was that just her anger?

She was flushed with it, trembling with it. And appalled by it. She had actually struck another human being. And if he hadn't caught her wrist, she would have struck him again. A gasp of shock at her own behavior slipped through her lips.

His blue eyes widened as he stared down at her. His face was close to hers—so close that she'd been sure he was going to kiss her. But he abruptly released her and stepped back, so quickly that she swayed slightly on her heels before regaining her balance.

She trembled, probably from the force with which her heart pounded in her chest and her pulse raced. With anger. It could only be anger. She hadn't actually wanted him to kiss her. He was beyond arrogant. He was obnoxious.

As if to prove it, he threw back his head and let out a loud laugh.

"I should have slapped you harder," she remarked. He'd certainly deserved it.

Still laughing, he shook his head. "I wasn't saying that to you."

She gestured at the room, which was empty but for the two of them and all those weights and machines. "I'm the only one here."

"But I didn't know you were the one who'd walked in," he said.

Her skin heated with embarrassment as she realized he spoke the truth. He'd been flat on his back on that bench, lifting the weight bar. He hadn't even glanced up before he'd spoken. He must've just known some-one had walked in because he'd heard her heels hitting the floor.

"You're the last person I expected to show up here," he continued.

So he had been expecting some other tense and edgy woman who couldn't wait for him to finish before getting laid. Not that she was tense and edgy.

Well, she was—but with outrage, not desire. Her gaze kept slipping, though, down to his chest. To all those muscles, his skin glistening with sweat. A bead trickled from between his pecs and trailed over wash-board abs to disappear into the waistband of his shorts.

Her throat suddenly very dry, she struggled to swal-low. And to pull her gaze up—back to his face. But that wasn't much better. His square jaw was dark with stubble, and his black hair, slick with moisture, clung to his muscled neck. Her fingers itched to touch his face again, but not to slap it. Then she met his eyes, saw the amusement there, and she reconsidered…slapping him.

"Why are you here, Fiona?" he asked, his mouth sliding into a slightly crooked, sexy-as-hell grin. Sounding almost hopeful, he added, "Are you feeling tense and edgy?"

She lifted her hand even though she had no intention of losing control enough to swing it. "Do you want me to slap you again?"

"Are you into that?" he asked and arched a black brow over one of those twinkling eyes. "I didn't figure you for the S&M scene. Didn't actually figure you for any scene. Didn't think sex was your thing…"

She didn't know what infuriated her more. That he'd thought about her and sex. Or that he'd thought about her not having sex. Ever.

She wasn't frigid. Not at all…

At the moment—standing too close to his sweat-slick, musky-smelling body—she wished she was, though. Then she wouldn't have noticed how muscular he was. Muscles bulged in his arms and chest and back. Did he spend all his time in the gym?

Or in some woman's bed?

His gaze skimmed down her body to her high heels. "But now I can see the whole dominatrix thing."

"I'm here because I'm mad," she admitted. If only she could have controlled her temper long enough to realize that it was pointless to try to talk to a man like Wyatt Andrews. He was infuriating. "And you're only making it worse."

"We aren't equipped to put out those kinds of fires here," he remarked.

"Pointless," she murmured as she spun on her heel to turn toward the door.

Long fingers wrapped around her arm, tightly enough that she jerked against his grasp as she tried to walk away.

"Wait, wait," he said. "I can try to help. Why are you mad?"

"Because of you."

He sighed. "I told you I didn't realize you were the one who'd walked in—"

"No, I'm not mad about that." Not anymore. Not now that she had calmed down enough to be rational. Of course he hadn't known who'd walked in. Since she'd driven over here anyway, she might as well talk to him. She drew in a deep breath to brace herself and turned back around to face him. "I want to talk to you about my brother."

His hand dropped from her arm and he stepped back. "Has he done something?"

"You know what he's done," she said. Since she was pretty sure it had been Wyatt's idea, or at least his influence. "He's dropped out of college in order to join the Forest Service Fire Department."

"So why, exactly—" he spoke slowly, as if he were dealing with someone unstable "—are you mad at me?"

"Because he wants to become *you*."

His mouth curved into that slightly crooked grin again. "You say that like it's a bad thing."

God, he was arrogant. But maybe he had a reason to be. He was sexy as hell—so sexy that women were apparently unable to wait to have sex with him.

"Pointless," she murmured again. "I made a mistake coming here. I can't reason with you." She could barely reason with herself at the moment—his bare skin and rippling muscles were too distracting.

"I don't know what you want to reason with me about," he said, "but I'm willing to talk to you."

Frustration gnawed at her. She had practiced her argument the entire drive across town. But now she could remember nothing of what she'd rehearsed.

"Let me shower first," he said, "and change. I'll meet you at the bar around the corner and you can reason with me."

She doubted that. "Why?" she asked.

He arched the brow again. "Why what?"

"Why are you willing to talk to me?" She'd expected the arrogance and the argument. She hadn't expected him to be open to reason or even to a conversation. "I thought you had a date."

She swallowed a groan as she remembered that she had one. She had intended to call Howard on the drive across town to cancel their date. But then she'd gotten distracted rehearsing what she would say when she confronted Wyatt Andrews. All those words had left her mind the moment he'd made his suggestive comment.

He glanced to the doorway behind her and remarked, "Here's my date now."

So much for that conversation. She doubted he would pass up a sure thing to instead just talk to a woman he'd figured was frigid. She turned around to leave and to check out his date. But a man—as tall and muscular as Wyatt—blocked the doorway. He was the one who had directed her where to find Wyatt.

The man laughed. "You should be so lucky as to date me."

Wyatt grinned. "You wouldn't turn me down," he said. "You're so tense and edgy, you'd definitely go home with me at the end of the night."

Both men laughed. But Fiona failed to see the humor. Her pulse quickened instead. Was Wyatt expecting her to go home with him at the end of the night?

"If you're busy…" They could do this another night. That didn't mean that he wouldn't expect her to go home with him that night, too.

"Have you changed your mind about making me listen to reason?" Wyatt teased.

The other man laughed again—harder. "If he's willing to listen to *reason*, you should take him up on that," he advised. "And we didn't actually have any plans. He's just messing with me."

Was he just messing with her, too? Probably. But she hadn't driven across town to just yell at him. Or slap him. She'd wanted to talk to him—to get him to help her. His influence was why Matthew had dropped out of college; he was the only one who could get her brother to change his mind and get his life back on track.

"The bar around the corner?" she asked. "Which way?"

"To the right," he said. "I'll be there before you finish your first drink."

She had no intention of drinking with him. And she definitely had no intention of going home with him.

She wanted only to talk.

But since she wasn't going to see him with so few clothes on again, she couldn't resist letting her gaze slip once more—over his chest and down his six-pack abs. She was definitely not drinking with him; she couldn't risk losing control. And because she never risked losing control, she hadn't built up a tolerance for alcohol. She was the proverbial lightweight when it came to drinking.

If she had too many drinks, she *might* go home with him. She jerked her attention away from all that naked flesh and muscle and turned toward the door.

"I'll be there right after I hit the shower," he promised.

And an image of him standing completely naked beneath a spray of water sprang to her mind. Her skin flushed again and heated more than it had with her temper. She quickened her step. Because of the heels, she couldn't run. But she had the urge to run—and to keep running.

THE WOMAN HAD some ass, wriggling inside that snug skirt as she walked away. But Wyatt wasn't the only one watching her leave. Braden actually craned his neck to stare as she turned outside the door and headed down the hall.

When she'd disappeared from sight entirely, the captain finally turned back to Wyatt and let out a low whistle. "I hate to admit it, but you might be right about me," he said. "What bar are you meeting her at? The Filling Station?"

It was the only bar around the corner. But Wyatt wasn't about to point that out to his boss. Feeling tense and edgy himself, he shook his head. "Not her."

Braden whistled again. "It's not like you to stake a claim. Thought you didn't get attached…"

"I'm not," he protested. "Not at all—especially not to Fiona."

"Fiona…" Braden murmured wistfully. Or lustfully…

Hearing the lust, Wyatt smacked the other man's shoulder. "Hey, she's a friend's sister, so she's off-limits." At least to him.

Braden snorted. "I've met the sister of every man on the team."

Wyatt believed it. Braden was the kind of superintendent who made it a point to meet the families of all his team members…though for a couple of them the team was the only family they had. Wyatt's parents had been killed when he was eleven. And another one of the guys—Cody Mallehan—had been an orphan, too.

Braden continued, "*She* is not related to any of them."

"I have friends outside the team." Because of the wives who had made them give up the jobs they had loved. But she wasn't related to any of them, either. "She's the sister of one of the kids I've been mentoring."

Except that Matt wasn't a kid anymore. So he should be able to make decisions without his sister's interference. Even if those decisions were wrong, he needed to figure it out for himself—not have someone berate him for it. Matt had told Wyatt that Fiona was bossy and controlling, which was part of the reason why the half siblings weren't close. The other part was that they hadn't been raised together.

"Then she's not off-limits to *me*," Braden pointed out. "I think I will join you at the bar."

Wyatt smacked him again—a little harder. "She's off-limits to you, too."

"I may have met most of the kids you mentor…"

Because Wyatt had brought them around the firehouse. He hoped he hadn't inadvertently influenced Matt's decision to try to join the Forest Service Fire Department.

"But I'm not friends with any of them," Braden continued.

"That's not why she's off-limits to you," Wyatt said. "She's off-limits because she's the type of woman you need to avoid."

"What type is that?" Braden asked. "Sexy as sin?"

"The type that wants you to make a commitment and then gives you ultimatums or walks away," Wyatt warned him. "And you've already had one of those."

Braden sighed. "It's not always the wife who gives the ultimatums, you know."

Wyatt narrowed his eyes and studied his friend. "Do you want to talk?" he asked. "I can cancel with Fiona…" But his stomach muscles tightened, his gut clenching in protest.

Why? She was probably just going to yell at him. She had been pissed even before he'd made his inappropriate comments to her.

"Maybe you should," Braden said.

So his friend was finally ready to talk—to *really* talk. He'd said some things before, when he and his wife had hit their rough patch. But he hadn't explained the situation and how it had led to a divorce so quickly.

"I will if you want me to," he offered. Selfishly he hoped that Braden didn't want him to. "I'll have to run over to the bar and let her know, though." Since he didn't have her number…

He'd known Matt for six years, but he'd barely ever seen or talked to the guy's sister. As Matt had said, they weren't close. So why was she so upset over his career aspirations?

"But then we can talk," Wyatt said. "As long as you want…"

Braden laughed. "I don't want to talk to you."

"Well, I was just kidding about the sex earlier," Wyatt joked. "You're not my type."

Braden smacked his shoulder now. "I'm just saying that maybe you need to take your own advice."

He was a little sexually frustrated himself—more so since Fiona O'Brien had walked into the weight room and slapped him. And he'd touched her…

He might have kissed her if she hadn't tried to hit him again. That had brought him to his senses. He had no business kissing a woman like Fiona, let alone having sex with her.

He shook his head. "No…"

"You're warning me to steer clear of women like her," Braden reminded him. "Maybe you should, too."

Wyatt laughed. "But I'm in no danger of falling for her." For any other woman, either, but most especially not a woman like Fiona. He wanted nothing to do with bossy and controlling.

"She's beautiful and sexy," Braden said. "Yeah, no danger at all…"

"No," Wyatt said again.

But moments later he turned the water cold as he stepped into the shower. After that passionate encounter with her, after nearly giving in to the temptation to kiss her, he needed to cool off. But no matter how cold the water was, his skin was still hot. His blood still pumping fast and hard through his veins.

She was beautiful and sexy. But he had known

plenty of women just as hot. And he hadn't fallen for any of them.

He was not going to fall for Fiona O'Brien.

3

"WHERE ARE YOU?" Howard asked, his voice squeaking in her ear. Not that he had a squeaky voice. It must have been the bad cell reception and the noise in the bar that made his voice sound so whiny and petulant.

Fiona considered walking out to finish the call on the street. But then she would lose the booth she'd found in the back of the crowded bar. And she would have to walk past all those guys who'd whistled at her when she'd walked in. Since she was one of the only women in the place, she hadn't been particularly flattered. The other woman was heavily muscled and tattooed and had also whistled at her.

She pressed her mouth against the phone and said, "I had to take a meeting."

"In a bar?" he asked. And there was definitely petulance in his tone.

She couldn't blame the cell reception. And she couldn't blame him for being upset that she had canceled. She should have been flattered that he was so disappointed. But was he disappointed or merely irritated?

Of course, she hadn't canceled until he was already on his way to the restaurant where they met every Friday night. A nice restaurant—not a place like this with a loud jukebox, louder patrons and peanuts crushed against the scarred wide-planked wooden floor.

"I'm sorry," she said. "But something's come up with Matthew—"

"Your brother." Now a sigh, one that sounded long-suffering, rattled the phone.

"I'm sorry," she said again. Did she talk that much about Matthew?

Sure, she was worried about her brother; she had been worried about him pretty much since the day he was born. She'd only been six at the time, but she was the one who'd rushed to him every time he'd cried. She was the one who had been there for him...until she'd been taken away. After her stepfather's death of a drug overdose, her paternal grandparents had decided her mother was unfit to raise their granddaughter. They'd sued her mother for custody of her and won— taking eleven-year-old Fiona away from her five-year-old brother.

Fiona wanted to be there for Matthew again. But he wouldn't let her. Maybe he resented that she'd left him. That hadn't been her choice, though. The judge hadn't listened to what she'd wanted. And now Matthew wouldn't listen to her, either. He only listened to Wyatt Andrews.

"Well, I'll let you get back to your meeting with him," Howard said.

She opened her mouth to correct his misassumption that she was with Matthew. Would he be jealous over her meeting another man in a bar, though—even if it was just to talk about her brother?

But before she could say more, he continued, "I'll see you next Friday."

"Why not before?" she asked.

Wyatt hadn't been talking to her when he'd been teasing about being edgy and tense. But he could have been.

She just hadn't been aware that she was…until she'd seen him, lifting weights—his naked arms and chest straining, muscles rippling, skin glistening with sweat. Her mouth dry again, she wondered where the drink was that she'd ordered when she'd walked in. And then it suddenly appeared on the table in front of her. She grabbed the glass and took a quick sip.

And gasped as the fiery liquid burned her throat. This wasn't the club soda she'd requested. It tasted more like gin than tonic water.

Howard was talking—something about busy schedules or sticking to schedules. She barely heard him as she looked up to tell the waitress that the bartender had gotten her drink wrong. Since she hadn't seen a waitress when she'd walked in, she'd given her order directly to him. But it wasn't a waitress who stood beside the booth.

It wasn't Wyatt, either. This man was nearly as tall and muscular, though. But while Wyatt's hair was dark and too long, this man's was light and clipped short. His eyes were light, too, a pale green. Was he a waiter? A different bartender from the one she'd spoken to?

"I'm sorry," she murmured.

Howard thought she was talking to him. "You've already apologized," he said. "I understand you need to talk to your brother. We'll see each other next week."

"Yes," she said. "Goodbye…"

Howard had already clicked off the phone. She did the same and dropped her cell back into her purse.

"I'm sorry," she said again to the man leaning over her booth—over her. She raised her voice so that he would hear her. "But this isn't the drink I ordered."

"I know," he said as he slid into the booth to sit across from her. "I ordered this drink for you." He held a frosted mug of beer, which he clinked against the glass she hadn't realized she was still holding. "Cheers to the most beautiful woman in the place."

She glanced around and discovered that the only other woman had left. And despite herself, she laughed.

He sucked in a breath. "*Beautiful* doesn't even do you justice."

Oh, God, she'd inadvertently encouraged him. She pushed the drink toward him. "No, thank you," she told him. For the drink and the compliment. "I'm waiting for someone."

"He's too late."

She wondered what was keeping Wyatt, and that damn image flashed through her mind again—of him standing naked in the shower, water sluicing over his skin and muscles…

Despite the sudden dryness in her throat, she didn't reach for the glass again. The last thing she needed was alcohol. Her judgment was already impaired, or she wouldn't keep thinking of Wyatt Andrews…*naked*.

"He'll be here soon," she said. But she really had no idea. Maybe this was a joke—sending the woman he apparently considered frigid into a bar full of men.

The guy sighed. "What a waste…" he remarked. "A woman like you waiting for an idiot like him."

"You don't know who I'm waiting for," she said. She considered Wyatt Andrews a lot of things: arrogant, reckless, insufferable. But he was no idiot.

"He's a fool for making a woman like you wait," he said. "I would never do that to you."

She was tempted to laugh again. But she'd already encouraged this man too much. So she assumed the icy demeanor she used to dissuade men like him—the same demeanor she'd previously used with Wyatt Andrews. No wonder he'd thought she was frigid. Hopefully this man would, too.

"You can keep your drink," she said, pushing it closer to him. "And your opinion."

He laughed now and held up his hands. "To inspire so much loyalty in you, this must be some amazing guy you're meeting."

"I am," a deep voice said—too close to her ear—as Wyatt Andrews slid into the booth to sit next to her. His hard body, smelling shower fresh, pressed against her side. Shoulder against shoulder, hip and thigh against hip and thigh.

Heat flashed through her. She was definitely not frigid. "There you are," she murmured.

Instead of taking the hint and leaving, the other man tipped back his head and laughed. "Wyatt. I should have known it was you she was waiting for."

"Why?" The question slipped out without her realizing it. But she wanted to know.

The blond guy readily replied, "Who else would have staked a claim on the most beautiful woman in the bar?"

"I'm the only woman," she reminded him. "And Wyatt has no claim on me."

"Well, if that's the case..." He pushed her drink across the narrow table.

She'd inadvertently encouraged him again. Maybe that was why she didn't protest when Wyatt slid his arm around her shoulders and tugged her closer—as if it were possible for them to get any closer.

No space separated their bodies.

She could feel his heart beating against the side of her breast. It was beating fast and hard. Unfortunately so was hers.

"Get lost, Cody," he told the other man. "I apparently have to stake my claim."

She turned her face toward him, to protest his arrogance. But her lips barely opened before his mouth covered hers. Like his body, it was hot and sexy. He took advantage of her parted lips to deepen the kiss, flicking his tongue inside her mouth.

Heat rushed through her. It wasn't anger. Or even embarrassment. It was desire.

Did he feel it, too? He slid his lips across hers, back and forth, and dipped his tongue inside once more, stroking over hers. Teasing her.

God, he was teasing her.

She realized it when he pulled back, and his blue eyes glittered as he stared at her. She was the idiot—not Wyatt. She glanced across the table to the man who'd called him that. But the blond guy was gone.

They were alone. And still much too close together.

"Are you going to slap me again?" he asked, almost hopefully.

So she lifted her hand to his face.

WYATT WAITED FOR the sting of her palm connecting with his skin. He needed a hard slap to snap him out of it—out of his gut-clenching desire for her. His body was hard and aching.

But instead, her fingertips glided along his jaw. "You'd like that too much," she said. "I did figure you for that S&M stuff."

"Not me," he protested. "I'm into pleasure—not pain." Being with her would certainly be pleasurable. She was so hot—so passionate. But being with her would also lead to pain—to commitments, to ultimatums.

Her fingers lingered on his chin, almost absently stroking along his jaw. "You didn't shave."

"I didn't want to keep you waiting too long." He glanced toward where Cody Mallehan stood at the bar. His team member and friend lifted his beer mug in a salute. "It looks like I was nearly too late."

"He said you were," she admitted as she glanced at the bar, too.

"He would," he said. "He thinks he's God's gift to women."

"He is good-looking," she murmured as she continued to look toward the bar and Cody.

Was she actually attracted to his friend? When Wyatt had found them in the booth at the back of the bar, she'd been acting all ice queen again.

"I thought he was bothering you," Wyatt said.

"So that's why you kissed me?" she asked. "To get rid of him?"

"Of course." But he nearly choked on the lie. He should have ordered a beer when he'd walked in; then he would have had something to wash it down with and something to cool off the desire still burning inside him. He had kissed her because he'd wanted to since she'd slapped him earlier. And now, after kissing her once, he wanted to kiss her again.

And more...

He wanted to do more than kiss her.

God, he needed a drink. He had no more than entertained the thought than a beer appeared at his elbow. He glanced up at the bartender who'd brought it over. Since Wyatt was a regular, the guy had probably known what he wanted. He reached for his wallet.

But the bartender shook his head. "Cody sent it over. He said you won this round." He slid a drink toward her, too. "And here's the club soda you ordered." He headed back toward the bar.

"Cody's not the only one who thinks he's God's gift," Fiona murmured. "You two have some kind of rivalry over women?"

"Over most things," Wyatt admitted. "We work together."

"Then thank you," she said, "for getting rid of him. I kept inadvertently encouraging him."

"Breathing is all the encouragement Cody needs to hit on a woman," Wyatt said. "But why does it matter that he works with me?"

Because she was interested in him?

She had kissed him back. Hadn't she? He'd been so into her—into tasting and feeling and exploring her mouth that he hadn't noticed if he'd been the only one feeling it. Feeling the desire. The passion...

She shuddered as if revolted. "I would *never* date a firefighter."

Pride stinging, he asked, "Why not?" Not that he wanted to date her. He didn't actually date, anyway.

"Too great a risk."

And that was why he didn't want to date her or women like her who considered his career too dangerous. He wanted the women who were attracted to the excitement and glamor of his job. And there were always plenty of them around. Not tonight, though.

He glanced around the bar and noticed it was men only. Where the hell were all the women?

"I'm taking off," Cody said as he stopped by their booth again. "This place is dead tonight. Everybody's at that new club opening across town."

Everybody except the regulars who worked in the immediate area.

"Why aren't you?" Wyatt asked.

Cody shrugged. "They're focusing on bringing in the female clientele."

"I repeat—why aren't you?"

"They're using male strippers to do that." Cody shuddered as Fiona had only moments earlier—with pure revulsion.

"Can't stand the competition?" Wyatt teased.

The other man shrugged. "I already lost once tonight." He glanced wistfully at Fiona. "It was nice meeting you."

She lifted her glass. "Thanks for the drink, but I prefer the club soda."

Cody pointed to Wyatt's glass. "I wouldn't have too many of those. Captain Zimmer has that feeling."

Wyatt nodded. "I know. He's all tense and edgy."

"A fire's gotta be getting started," Cody said. "Somewhere…"

A fire was, but it was inside Wyatt, a burning desire for a certain redhead.

"It's too cold around here. So it's gotta be out west," Cody said—almost hopefully. Travel was likely the part Cody enjoyed most about being a Hotshot. Probably because the guy was rarely able to stay in one place for very long. "I'm going back to the firehouse to check in with him." He nodded at Fiona again before turning away.

She looked a little wistful as she watched Cody walk out of the bar.

Something tightened Wyatt's stomach muscles into a knot again, but it wasn't desire this time. It was something that Wyatt didn't recognize because he'd never felt it before—at least not until he'd caught Braden watching her walk away earlier. Jealousy?

"He's gone," she said.

"Yeah…"

She shoved against his side. "You can move to the other side of the booth."

It would have been the smart thing to do—to get some distance between them so that he stopped torturing himself with her closeness, with her heat…

And Wyatt always did the smart thing. That was why his job wasn't overly dangerous. Like all of the forest service firefighters on the specialized team called Hotshots, he was well trained, and he knew what he was doing. The same went for Wyatt's personal life— he knew what he was doing and never got into a situation that would put his heart or his livelihood at risk. But he didn't move. In fact he leaned a little closer to her, his lips nearly brushing her ear. She smelled fresh and flowery, and he breathed in her scent like he breathed in air.

"It's loud in here," he pointed out. The bartender must have turned up the jukebox; Wyatt would have to make sure to leave him a tip. "We'll have to shout if I move across the table." As he spoke, his lips did brush over her ear.

And she shuddered. He didn't think it was with revulsion this time. No. He wasn't the only one who'd felt the desire.

"It is loud in here," she agreed.

He grinned. Obviously, she didn't want him to move, either.

But then she continued, "Too loud to talk."

"We could go to my place," he offered. "It's close." And he was an idiot for suggesting it. What had happened to his usual sense of self-preservation?

She shook her head, and the lock of hair that had escaped that tight knot on the back of her head brushed across his jaw. He shuddered now as his body reacted to the touch of silk against his skin.

He should have been relieved that she'd refused his offer—that she realized what a bad idea it was, too. But disappointment slowed his racing pulse. "I thought you wanted to talk about Matt."

A little line formed between her reddish brows. "I do. I want to talk about his crazy idea to quit college and become a firefighter."

He tilted his head and furrowed his brow—as if he was having trouble hearing her. "Crazy what?" he asked.

"Decision to become a firefighter," she said. "And not just any firefighter, he wants to become a Hotshot."

That was crazy. Seriously crazy. "We do need to talk," he said. "But we can't do it here."

She leaned closer now—as if she hadn't heard him that clearly, either. Her brow furrowed again, and he could see the indecision in her green eyes. "I really want to talk…"

"So come home with me," he urged her. The urgency was all his, clamoring inside him with that desire. "Come home with me…"

4

"HE WANTED ME to go home with him." Outrage coursed through Fiona as she raised her voice loud enough to be heard over the blaring music that pulsed throughout the new club. Were there no quiet places left in the usually sleepy town?

Tammy leaned across the glass and neon bar to wave down the bartender with a twenty, like all the other women vying for drinks. She turned back to remark, "Maybe you should have."

Fiona gasped—though she shouldn't have been surprised. Tammy never turned down an opportunity to enjoy herself. And she would have enjoyed herself with Wyatt Andrews.

Fiona might have—if she'd been able to forget who and what he was and just focus on all those sleek muscles and his lips...

They'd tasted of decadence and had been as intoxicating as the drink his friend had bought her. What would they have felt like on other parts of her body?

She shook her head—shaking off Tammy's suggestion and her own temptation. And she had been tempted—so tempted that instead of thinking to suggest a quieter place to talk, she'd made an excuse and hurried from the loud bar to a louder bar. "That's crazy..."

As crazy as her coming here—to a nightclub full of tipsy women drooling over male strippers. But she'd wanted to vent to her friend about what a jerk Wyatt Andrews was, and Tammy had already been pulling into the parking lot of this place. Her friend was dressed in a bright yellow dress—meant to draw the attention of every man in the place. Unfortunately for Tammy, the crowd was predominantly female.

If Wyatt had wanted just a hookup for the night, he should have come here—instead of meeting her at the neighborhood bar. Maybe he had only intended to talk to her. But then why hadn't he suggested a quiet coffee shop? Why his home?

The bartender took Tammy's twenty, but the pretty brunette shook her head to refuse a drink. She only wanted change. Moments later she victoriously held up her handful of dollars. With her free hand, she grabbed Fiona's and tugged her along as she headed toward the dance floor.

The place was all neon and glittering black surfaces and glass. It glowed with bright colors—which made Tammy blend in while Fiona, still dressed in the beige suit from work, stood out.

She tried to dig in her heels and stop Tammy from dragging her along. But her friend was freakishly strong. Or Fiona was a wimp. She was going with Tammy whether she wanted to or not. And she didn't want to.

At all.

She had been more tempted to go home with Wyatt

Andrews. He may have just wanted to talk. These guys wanted tips and seemed willing to do anything—or *anyone*—in order to get them.

Men danced among all the women on the floor. Or they danced around them, gyrating and pulling off their costumes as they did. The women danced with the male strippers and clapped and cheered. Some laughed, some giggled and shrieked.

Fiona watched in disgust. This might be other women's fantasies, but to her, and the life insurance agent in her, it was a bad joke. All those good-looking men were dressed as the most hazardous professions—police officers, marines, navy SEALS, race car drivers, construction workers, FBI agents and, of course, firemen.

Tammy danced with the firefighter, and as she did, she slid dollar bills into the waistband of the pants hanging low on his lean hips. Of course, he wore no shirt, just suspenders stretched over his waxed and shiny chest. He wasn't nearly as muscular as Wyatt. But then he wasn't a real firefighter. He wasn't Wyatt. While he swiveled his hips for Tammy, he winked at Fiona. He was probably only flirting because he wanted money from her, too. Why had Wyatt flirted with her? Just to mess with her?

Eventually, Tammy ran out of dollar bills and tugged Fiona's hand to pull her back to the bar. "This time I actually need a drink," she said, fanning herself. "You?"

Fiona already felt as if she'd had too much to drink, even though she'd only taken a sip of that gin and tonic. Why else hadn't she slapped Wyatt Andrews for kissing her as boldly as he had? Why had she thought about, for just that fleeting moment, going home with him?

Because of Matthew. She needed to talk to Wyatt about her brother.

"Red wine?" Tammy asked.

Fiona shook her head. "Nothing."

"You don't have to work in the morning," Tammy reminded her. "Which is another reason you should have gone home with the hunky firefighter."

Just because tomorrow was Saturday didn't mean she wasn't working. She liked going in when the office was closed so she could catch up without interruptions.

"You haven't met Wyatt," Fiona reminded her. "And that guy on the dance floor is not a real firefighter."

"So Wyatt isn't hunky?"

She couldn't lie, so she just pretended not to hear her friend. The music was loud…

But Tammy knew her too well and laughed. "You need to get some, girl."

"I'm seeing Howard."

Tammy laughed again. "Like I said, you need to get some."

"I would *never* get involved with a man like Wyatt Andrews." She was not her mother's daughter. She would not go for excitement over substance. For fleeting over forever…

Both of her mother's husbands had been on that dance floor. Not the real men. They were dead. But their professions had been represented. Fiona's father had been a race car driver—albeit just dirt tracks— and Matthew's had been a rock star wannabe in a band that had done more drugs than gigs. The hazards of both those jobs had killed them. Speed had killed her father; he had been driving too fast when he'd hit the wall. And heroin had killed Matthew's; the wannabe rock star had been living too fast.

Now the brunette shook her head. "You don't have to get *involved* with him. You could just enjoy him."

"What's to enjoy?" Fiona asked. But she knew— she had enjoyed that kiss. She shouldn't have, though. She shouldn't have forgotten what he was really like. "He's arrogant and obnoxious. And he's going to get my brother killed."

"That's why you should have gone home with him," Tammy said.

She gasped in shock over her friend's remark.

Tammy winked. "Maybe you could have convinced him to refuse Matt a recommendation. Hell, if you're really good, maybe you could convince him to tear up the application altogether."

"What are you suggesting?"

Tammy shrugged. "Hey, you know my motto—work what your mama gave you…" She wriggled her ass as she made the comment.

Fiona's mother hadn't given her many physical attributes. Except for some of her delicate facial features, she looked more like her father's family—like her paternal grandmother. But Fiona was afraid that her mother might have passed along her bad taste in men. Why else had Fiona been so attracted to a man like Wyatt Andrews? To a Hotshot?

The first time Matthew had mentioned his mentor to her, Fiona had looked up the definition of a Hotshot. He was like the soldier on the front line. He was the one who got closest to the blaze. While other people battled it from above, in helicopters and planes dumping water on it. The Hotshots were the ones on the ground trying to starve the fire to extinguish it.

Fiona asked her outrageous friend, "Are you suggesting I use sex to get what I want?"

Tammy laughed. "Don't look so horrified. Women do it all the time."

Fiona opened her mouth, but no words came out. She didn't know if she was insulted for just herself or for all women. "I haven't..."

Tammy leaned in and nudged her shoulder. "But since you're such a prude, you wouldn't have to actually have sex with him. Just make him think you would if he'd get Matt to change his mind about the whole firefighter thing and go back to college."

Fiona tilted her head as she considered her friend's suggestion. For Matt, she was tempted to try it. "There's only one problem with your plan..."

Tammy arched a dark brow. "Yes?"

"What if he doesn't want to have sex with me?"

Tammy snorted. "Why do you think he wanted you to go home with him? To play cards?"

"He said to talk." And maybe that was all he had wanted to do, talk about Matt. But then she'd chickened out—because of that kiss, because of how it had made her feel.

Tammy snorted again. "If you believed that, you would have gone home with him."

It wasn't him she'd been concerned about, though. She'd worried that if they were alone at his place, that *she* might want to do more than talk. But that was crazy. No matter how sexy he was or how exciting his kiss, she didn't want anything to do with a man like him.

But for Matthew…

She had to try to talk to Wyatt Andrews again. Had to convince him to help her change Matthew's mind. And if talking to Wyatt didn't work, maybe she would actually consider Tammy's suggestion.

"Who's all tense and edgy now?" Braden teased Wyatt.

He shrugged, trying to ease the tension that kissing Fiona had wound tightly inside him. "It must be all your talk about a fire…"

Or a fiery redhead.

The grin slid off Braden's face. "It's out there…"

Wyatt didn't doubt him. He could almost feel it himself now. "*You* have to get out there," he said. "That's why I brought you here."

But he paused outside the door to the new club, reluctant to step inside. Cody was right; the place was packed. That was why he'd brought Braden here—because of all the women. Usually he would have been interested himself. But he doubted anyone inside the club could make his pulse race as Fiona had. If only she'd gone home with him.

But it was a good thing that she hadn't. He didn't need to get involved with a woman like her. He didn't need bossy and controlling. He just needed a good time. Maybe he'd find one inside.

"We might as well check it out," he told his boss.

The bouncer holding open the door gave him and Braden a quick once-over. "I thought all the dancers were already inside."

"Dancers?" Braden repeated with confusion.

Wyatt hadn't shared everything Cody had told him

about the club opening. If his boss had known about the male strippers, he never would have agreed to check out the place.

Braden hadn't gone many steps inside before he turned around and slammed into Wyatt. "This was a bad idea. I'm leaving." But before he could get anywhere near the door, two women grabbed his arms and pulled him onto the dance floor.

Wyatt laughed at the look of horror on his friend's face. Maybe he should have advised Braden to change out of the Huron Hotshots Firefighter T-shirt he was wearing with khakis. But the women would soon realize their mistake when they discovered that Braden couldn't dance.

His boss was going to kill him. But at least Wyatt was getting a good laugh before he died.

If Wyatt bought him a drink, Braden might loosen up, and maybe after a few drinks he would forget that coming here had been Wyatt's idea. He turned toward the bar. Despite the crowd around it, his gaze went immediately to the bright flame of her red hair.

It wasn't Fiona. Not here…

But he couldn't mistake that particular shade of red. Or the alabaster of her silky skin. She'd said she was going home, but she was here.

All her hair was loose and flowing around her shoulders now. And one of the dancers had strayed from the floor. Shirtless but for suspenders and yellow pants, the faux firefighter leaned close to her, trapping her between his naked chest and the bar.

Anger coursed through Wyatt along with a fresh flash of jealousy, a feeling he'd been unfamiliar with until tonight—until his friends had checked out Fiona. This man was no friend and definitely no firefighter.

Wyatt hurried over to her. His grip probably a little too hard, he grabbed the man's shoulder and peeled him off her. The guy whirled toward him with a glare.

"What's your problem?" the dancer asked.

Fiona was his problem.

But instead of admitting that, Wyatt asked his own question. "Aren't you supposed to be out on the dance floor?"

"Break," the guy replied. But he glanced nervously around before returning his attention to Fiona. "I have time for a drink."

She shook her head. "I already said no."

Ignoring Wyatt, the guy moved in on her again—thrusting his waxed chest in her face. "But—"

This time Wyatt grabbed him even harder and jerked him away from Fiona. Raising his voice to be heard above the din of conversation and the blare of the music, he shouted, "The lady said no."

The dancer snorted. "Lady? There isn't a lady in this place."

Instinct and anger had Wyatt pulling back his fist to swing. But before he could, silky hands locked around his forearm. "Don't…"

The dancer grinned. "You don't want him to hurt my handsome face."

She snorted now and said, "I don't want him to hurt his hand."

"I wouldn't hurt my hand," Wyatt assured her. Maybe Braden was right about him being the frustrated one now, because he really wanted to hit the jerk.

"I would tear you apart," the man threatened, but he glanced around nervously—as if looking for backup.

Wyatt never had to look; he always knew his team had his back. But he didn't need them now. He laughed at the other man's claim, and Fiona's grasp on his arm tightened. His skin heated and tingled beneath her silky touch, distracting him so much that he nearly missed the dancer winding up to swing. But he easily dodged the blow.

And the guy stumbled forward and almost fell. He'd obviously already had a drink, or several, himself. He hadn't needed another.

Maybe he needed a slap upside the head to sober him up. But recognizing it wouldn't be a fair fight, Wyatt stepped back, and unfortunately Fiona's hands fell away from his arm.

All icy dominatrix, Fiona pointed the dancer back to the floor. "Break's over…"

The guy shivered at her tone and turned away.

"Maybe I didn't need to come to your rescue," Wyatt mused.

She lifted her chin and glared at him. "I didn't need rescuing."

"Yet I keep finding you fighting off advances in bars," he said. He gestured around at the bustling club. "Didn't expect to see you here."

"I'm not," she said, and turned to push her way through the crowd.

Wyatt followed, his gaze dropping to her ass wriggling inside that tight skirt as she hurried to the exit. "Sure looks like you…" He would know that ass anywhere.

She brushed past the bouncer as she stepped through

the door. The man whistled in appreciation and nudged Wyatt's shoulder. She glanced back to glare at them both before stalking across the parking lot. Wyatt lengthened his stride to keep pace with her. "You don't have to follow me."

"I have to make sure you make it safely to your car," he said. "Don't know who else might try to buy you a drink on your way there…"

She shook her head, and her hair flowed around her shoulders. "He didn't want to buy *me* a drink," she said, and her pale skin flushed with embarrassment. "He wanted me to buy *him* one."

"He didn't need any more."

She nodded. "That's what I thought."

"Thought you weren't here," he reminded her. "But now I understand why you wouldn't come home with me—even though you claimed that you have to get up early in the morning."

"I do." She stopped beside a silver sedan and squeezed her keyless remote. The locks clicked and the lights flashed. He recognized the make and model for having the highest safety rating. He'd thought she hadn't come home with him because she wasn't attracted, but maybe she was playing it safe.

Though he'd found her at this club—where she'd known there would be male dancers… Another stupid twinge of jealousy struck him.

"But you couldn't resist stopping here to check out the male strippers," he said.

She laughed as if the idea was utterly ridiculous. "I just stopped here to talk to a friend."

"That guy's a friend?"

She shook her head. "Tammy is female."

"Tammy wasn't with you at the bar," he pointed out. Not that he would have noticed anyone but Fiona. He reached out to open her door for her. But he just held the handle, his arm stretched in front of her. Then he leaned closer and braced his other hand against the roof of her car, loosely encircling her. She lifted her hand and pressed it against his chest. "I thought you weren't into firefighters…"

She pushed against his chest, the warmth of her palm penetrating the thin layer of his shirt to his skin beneath. "I'm not…"

Had he imagined earlier that she'd kissed him back? Had it just been wishful thinking on his part? Temptation tugged at him, joining the tension. He wanted to lean down a little farther and brush his mouth across hers—to see if she tasted as sweet as he'd thought. To see if he'd imagined the heat and the passion…

Her breath caught as she stared up at him. Maybe she'd seen the hunger in his gaze. "That's why I didn't go home with you…"

He stepped back and lifted his hands. "Hey, I just wanted to talk. I thought that's what you wanted, too—to talk about your brother."

"I do," she insisted. "Even if you don't agree with me that the job he wants is too dangerous, you have to agree that it's crazy Matthew quit school when he applied to the forest service. He might not even get in."

It was clear that she didn't want him to.

"The kid might have acted rashly," he admitted.

"And the whole firefighter thing," she said, "that's ridiculous enough. But to want to become a Hotshot, too…"

Wyatt had a lot of pride in his job. And her disdain

for it stung. "If you actually wanted to talk to me about this," he said, "you should have come to my house." He gestured back at the building. "Instead you came here to pick up exotic dancers."

Her eyes narrowed, and he braced himself for another slap or to dodge a blow as he had in the club. But she laughed instead. "I came here to talk to a friend," she repeated. "She was the one preoccupied with the dancers."

And Fiona was preoccupied with her brother. He saw the worry on her face, and he'd heard it earlier in her voice. Beneath her anger with him, there was fear. "You can talk to me," he said, "about Matt…"

"Thank you."

Maybe he could get her to go home with him now— just to talk, of course. He opened his mouth to issue the invitation when a voice called out from the club. "Hey!"

He turned to the bouncer.

"Your friend's in trouble in here."

He groaned. Braden was going to kill him. But maybe he'd also saved him—from doing something crazy, such as being alone with Fiona O'Brien. Because Wyatt knew that if they were alone—truly alone—he wouldn't be able to resist temptation. He would have to kiss her again.

5

A DOOR CREAKED, jerking Fiona awake. She blinked her eyes open and tried to focus. The computer screen in front of her had gone black. How long had she been asleep?

Her brother, Matthew, stood in the doorway to her office, watching her. Whenever she looked at him, she saw a child—the towheaded toddler she'd had to leave when her grandparents had been awarded custody of her. But he'd grown up. He was tall and so broad that he nearly filled her doorway. His curls had turned dishwater blond, and there was none of the adoration with which he used to look at her in his brown eyes.

"This is what you want for me?" he asked with a shudder of revulsion. "A desk job so boring that you can't even stay awake?"

The desk job wasn't why she couldn't stay awake. She blamed Wyatt Andrews for that, as she did for so many other things—such as her younger brother's attitude and poor decisions. Every time she'd closed her eyes the night before, she'd seen Wyatt's face and his bare chest and sculpted abs...

She'd even been able to feel his mouth moving sensuously, hungrily over hers. How could she blame her brother for letting Wyatt Andrews get to him when the man had so easily gotten to her, as well?

"I haven't told you to get a desk job," she said. She knew that wasn't for everyone. She couldn't imagine Wyatt Andrews behind a desk—but she had imagined him last night—in other places. Like the backseat of her car...

Her bed...

Heat flashed through her, and she wished for a glass of ice water instead of the cup of lukewarm coffee sitting on the linen blotter on her driftwood-colored desk.

Resentment tugged her brother's mouth into a grimace. "It's what you want, though."

"I want you to finish college," she said. "And to choose a profession that's right for you." Not for Wyatt Andrews.

Matthew stuck out his chest and stabbed it with his thumb. "Being a Hotshot," he said. "That's right for me."

"Why?" she asked. "I looked it up." Years ago. "I know how dangerous it is—even more dangerous than being a regular firefighter."

It was also incredibly physically demanding—which explained why her formerly scrawny brother had started working out so strenuously. She'd thought that, too, had been his trying to emulate Wyatt. She just hadn't realized how much.

He shrugged. "You wouldn't understand..."

"Why you want to risk your life?" She shook her head. "No, I don't understand that." She stood up and came around her desk. But when she reached out for him, he stepped back. "Do you know what it would do to Mom if something happened to you?"

Losing her husbands had nearly destroyed her. Losing her son definitely would.

He snorted derisively. "Do you? You're the one who never sees her."

"I see her…" But it was difficult because the woman continued to make poor decisions. She kept dating men like her late husbands. Men who drove too fast and drank too much. She'd probably buried a few of them, too, but had refrained from admitting it to Fiona.

She wouldn't have wanted to hear "I told you so."

Matthew's mouth twisted into a grimace of disgust. "Then you know that Mandy would just drink an extra bottle of wine and forget all about me."

"I wouldn't." She reached out again, trying to stroke his hair as she'd done when they were kids. But he was too tall now. She could only squeeze his shoulder.

His grimace became a sneer of resentment. "You did."

She shook her head and reminded him, "It wasn't my choice to leave. You know that." According to the judge, she had been too young at eleven to make her own decision. But even then she'd known herself better than anyone else had. And she'd known that Matthew, at five, needed her more than her grandparents did.

He sighed. "I know. I know…"

"And I never forgot about you." She had visited as often as she'd been allowed and her mother had been able to afford. Her grandparents, who'd lived, and still lived, in Florida, had made certain the judge made her mother responsible for her travel expenses. They'd known it would keep her visits home to a minimum.

He laughed. "Maybe it would be better if you had forgotten about me."

She gasped.

"I'm just joking," he said.

But she wondered.

"You do tend to forget that I'm not that little kid you left," he said. There was nothing little about him now; he towered over her. "You can't boss me around anymore, sis."

"I don't want to boss you," she assured him. "I just want you to—"

"Do what *you* want," he finished for her.

"That's not the case at all," she said. She wanted him to finish college, but before she could explain, knuckles tapped against the open door behind Matthew.

"Hello?" Wyatt Andrews called out. "There wasn't anyone at the reception desk."

Fiona regretted now that she'd been so tired she'd forgotten to lock the outside door. She hadn't minded Matthew coming inside, but she would have rather not seen Wyatt Andrews again.

"Hey, Wyatt!" Matt turned around and grabbed the bigger man in a tight embrace. And there was that adoration with which he used to look at Fiona when they were kids.

Wyatt flinched and eased back. And Fiona gasped at the bruise on his handsome face.

"What the hell happened to you?" Matt asked.

Wyatt shrugged. "Bar fight…"

"I should've been there," her brother said. "I would've had your back."

"You're not twenty-one," she reminded him. He was too young to be in a bar, much less in a bar fight. He was also much too young to decide on a career that could cost him his life.

Matthew glared at her before turning back to his idol. "I'm sure the other guy looks worse."

"Guys," Wyatt corrected him.

And encouraged him. Fiona could almost see her brother's admiration grow. She was right in thinking that Wyatt had influenced Matthew's decision. Matthew didn't just want to be like him; he wanted to *be* him.

"What was the fight about?" Matthew asked. "Did you steal someone's girl?"

"I didn't steal anyone," Wyatt said. And he glanced at her over her brother's shoulder.

Matthew laughed and playfully punched his shoulder. "You wouldn't have to—all the women just want to be with you because you're a Huron Hotshot!"

Wyatt turned the bruised side of his face toward them. "And I thought it was because I'm so damn good-looking…"

He was—even with the bruise. It had done nothing to detract from his appeal. If anything, it had added to his attractiveness, giving him that air of danger women like Fiona's mother craved. But not Fiona…

"No sensible woman would want to get involved with a man who constantly risks his life," Fiona said. So where had her sense gone? Why had she let images of Wyatt Andrews keep her awake all night?

Matthew snorted. "Who wants sensible women?"

Definitely not a twenty-year-old kid. And probably not a thirty-year-old playboy firefighter who got into bar brawls. Tammy had been crazy to think Fiona would be able to use her limited feminine wiles to influence Wyatt to help her.

But she needed help. She wouldn't be able to convince Matthew on her own. If anything, her objections seemed to make him more determined to follow through with his dangerous plan.

"What are you doing here?" Matthew asked. He glanced nervously from one of them to the other.

Fiona had been wondering that herself. She doubted he'd lain awake thinking about her. Hell, he probably hadn't gone home alone—after he'd returned to the club to help his friend. He'd definitely been the most attractive man in the place.

Wyatt shrugged broad shoulders. "I have an appointment to talk…"

They hadn't made an official appointment. They hadn't had time before he'd rushed back inside the club.

Matthew turned to her, and his brown eyes narrowed with suspicion. "What are you doing?"

She gestured toward her desk. "Working…" It was what she was usually doing—making sure people were protected. That was what she was trying to do for Matthew, but he wouldn't appreciate her protection. He would see it only as interference.

"Yeah," Wyatt agreed. "I'm here to talk insurance."

The suspicion didn't leave Matthew's eyes—even as he turned to look at his idol. "Like you would ever worry about being insured…"

"I didn't agree to buy anything," Wyatt said. "I just agreed to talk." He glanced at his watch. "But I don't have much time."

Matthew looked between them again. He obviously wasn't buying that Wyatt had come to her office for an insurance appointment. But he respected him too much to call him a liar.

He respected him so much that he would listen to him—if Fiona could make Wyatt listen to her. She had to make him listen.

Matthew shot her a glare before he turned and headed out the door. He patted Wyatt's shoulder as he passed him. "I'll catch you later."

He made no promises to see her again. His showing up at her office had been unusual. But he'd known his call, telling her that he'd dropped out of college to become a firefighter, had upset her the day before. Had he come to check on her? Or had he been worried about what she might have done to stop him?

Like Wyatt?

Would she do *him* in order to stop her brother?

She turned her attention to him and where he now leaned against her doorjamb. She saw him as she had the night before in her dreams, as she had in the gym: bare-chested, muscles rippling, perspiration beading on his skin...

Maybe doing him wouldn't be such an extreme sacrifice after all. Not that she actually would. She was already dating someone. But she had never dreamed about Howard the way she had Wyatt. In fact, their relationship had been in limbo for so long that maybe it was time she ended it. Not for Wyatt, though. Not because of those decadent dreams...

THE INTENSITY OF Fiona's stare slightly unnerved Wyatt. Like he usually did when he was uncomfortable, he started goofing around. Lifting his hand to his bruised jaw, he asked, "Is there something on my face?" She hadn't been staring at his face, though. His fingers brushed the swollen flesh. "A smudge?"

"A fist-size bruise." She stepped closer and her fingers replaced his, skimming along his jaw. Instead of sympathy, her lips curved in amusement. "Did the dancer do this?"

He snorted. "And risk breaking a nail? No…"

"So what happened after I left the club?"

"My captain got in a fight on the dance floor."

"With the dancers?"

He shook his head, and now the amusement was all his. "No, with a couple of women who thought he was a dancer and were trying to take off his clothes."

"So how'd you get hit?" she asked.

"I gallantly stepped in to save my captain," he said. "And I got hit with a shoe."

She gasped. "Someone kicked you?"

He'd probably have a bigger bruise had that happened. "No, she swung it at me. It had a very large and hard wooden sole. Felt like getting whacked with a baseball bat."

She nodded. "Must've been a wedge."

"I don't know what it was," he replied. "Just that it hurt like hell."

"Not quite the bar fight you led Matthew to believe," she admonished him.

He shrugged. "I just let him assume."

"You said that he should see the other guys." She called him on his lie.

He shrugged. "And he should. He'd probably think they were cute. Maybe a little burly for women…"

She laughed. "If that's what you have to tell yourself in order to protect your fragile ego…"

He lowered his brows and fake glowered at her. "Hey, it did hurt like hell."

She rose up on tiptoe and replaced her fingertips with her mouth. "Poor baby," she murmured, her breath as soft and silky as her lips against his skin. She pressed a quick kiss to the bruise and stepped back.

He curled his hands into fists and held them at his sides so that he wouldn't reach for her—so that he wouldn't pull her against him and kiss her back.

He wanted to kiss her again—the way he had in the Filling Station. He needed to feel her lips moving beneath his. But that wasn't why he had come to her office; at least that wasn't what he had admitted to himself.

She turned away from him and walked back to her desk. He couldn't help watching her hips sway. Even though the office wasn't officially open, she was dressed as if it was. Another little suit with a tight skirt and high heels. She'd even bound her hair into a sexy knot on top of her head again. He wasn't sure if he preferred it that way or down around her shoulders.

Hell, he'd prefer it best spread across his pillow.

"You misled Matthew about your reason for being here, too," she said.

He shrugged. "Maybe not…maybe I realized that I am woefully underinsured."

"Oh, I'm sure you are," Fiona readily agreed. "But you're the last person I would insure."

"Why?" He pulled out his wallet and glanced inside. "Funny how my money looks the same as anyone else's."

"Even if I would insure you, you wouldn't be able to afford the premium." She stared at him as she had moments ago—with an intensity that slightly unnerved him. She sighed now, almost as if she was disappointed. "You're too great a risk…"

Somehow he suspected she wasn't talking about insurance anymore. But that wasn't what he'd intended to speak to her about anyway. Still, he was intrigued. "Why am I too great a risk?"

"Statistics show that men in your profession are very likely to die on the job."

He flinched. "I've been doing this a long time and never even had a close call." Of course, that all depended on one's definition of *close*. He suspected his differed from hers.

She replied, "There have been so many deaths, though, among regular firefighters—"

"I'm not a regular firefighter."

"And even more among Hotshots and smoke jumpers."

He knew the horrible tragedy that had skewed those statistics—where a whole team had died when a fire had shifted. He couldn't argue those statistics, not when lives—heroic lives—had been lost. And unfortunately they weren't the only Hotshots who'd died trying to save others.

"That's why Matthew has to go back to college," she said. "He needs to get a degree—"

Because here their opinions did not differ, Wyatt nodded. "I agree. I have one myself."

Her eyes widened slightly with obvious surprise.

"You thought I started fighting fires while I was still in high school?"

She shrugged. "I didn't know…"

"I did," he replied. "When I turned sixteen, I started

working summers for the forest service while I finished high school and college. I have a degree in psychology."

"How does that help you fight fires?"

"You'd be surprised…" he murmured. There was a lot she didn't know about him. But he'd enlightened her as much as he intended.

"So you agree that Matthew should finish college?"

"Is that why you wanted to talk to me?" he asked. "To get me to agree with you?"

She furrowed her brow and stared at him as if he was an idiot. "Well, yeah…"

He laughed at her honesty.

"Why did you agree to talk to me?"

Because he'd wanted to see her again. Because he'd wanted to kiss her again. But he wasn't about to admit to those reasons. "Because you're worried about your brother."

Her breath caught, and he saw that worry dim the brightness of her eyes. "Yes, I am."

"You should be," he admitted.

Her eyes widened in surprise. "I thought you'd stick up for him—that you would try to assure me that being a firefighter isn't too dangerous for him."

"It isn't," Wyatt said. "The forest service trains their firefighters very well. And nobody makes the Hotshot team until they're ready." And it could take years for someone to be ready. Most never were—even after they'd taken the jobs. So many burned out.

It was grueling work. But he loved it.

"If you don't think it's dangerous, why do you think I should be worried about him?" she asked.

He shivered as if there was a sudden chill in the air.

"That's how it felt being in here with the two of you—like January on Lake Huron."

"He resents me," she admitted.

"He's going to resent you more if you keep interfering in his life." That was his fear; it was why Wyatt had kept so many of his opinions to himself regarding Matt. He hadn't wanted to alienate the kid. He couldn't help him if the kid refused to talk to him.

Since he'd turned eighteen, Matt could have ended their association entirely. But they'd remained friends. It was, in fact, all Matt considered him now.

"I'm not interfering in his life," she said.

He arched a brow.

"I'm trying to save it," she said.

"I told you that the job's not dangerous." Especially not for Matt. There was no way he would ever be doing it. But Wyatt hesitated from sharing that with her. He wasn't involved in hiring, had nothing to do with the application process, so he wasn't supposed to comment on it. Braden always warned that there could be legal ramifications if anyone said too much about it. But the job wasn't the real issue between the siblings anyhow.

She shook her head. "Then how come so few insurance companies will underwrite firefighters or police officers for disability or life insurance? Statistics have proven that those professions are too dangerous."

People from other professions died, too. He knew that all too well. But he never shared his sad story with anyone; he didn't like to think about it much. So he just shrugged. "And insurance agents never die? They don't get in car accidents?"

"Not when they drive safe vehicles carefully."

He'd been right about her car; it had been a Top

Safety Pick—chosen by the Insurance Institute of Highway Safety. They had probably come to that decision based on statistics, too.

He grinned. "Do you ever take a risk?"

Her eyes widened again. She looked both surprised and fearful at the thought. Or maybe it was at his sudden closeness as he stepped away from the doorjamb to close the distance between them. "What do you mean?"

He leaned across her desk, his face close to hers, and asked, "Do you ever drive over the speed limit? Accept a drink from a stranger?"

She shook her head so vehemently a strand of red hair slipped free of that knot.

"That's too bad…" He emitted a pitying sigh. "You don't know what you're missing…" He wanted to show her. That was why he leaned a little closer—close enough to brush his mouth across hers.

Her breath shuddered out, warm and silky against his lips. And her thick lashes drifted down as her eyes closed. He deepened the kiss—as much as he could with a desk between them. He wanted to kick it aside; he wanted nothing between his body and hers. His tongue slipped inside her mouth; he thrust it deep, like he wanted to thrust inside her. He groaned at the thought.

And she jerked back as if she'd just awakened. Her chair creaked as it rolled her away from the desk— away from him. "I asked to meet with you just to talk," she said.

He sighed again. "That's too bad…"

"You admit you're worried about Matthew, too."

"I'm worried that you're going to try to manipulate and control him, and you'll totally alienate him."

He was a little worried that she might do the same to him—manipulate and control. He wasn't certain that even her doing that could alienate him, though. He narrowed his eyes and studied her with the same suspicion her brother had.

"I love my brother," she said.

He nodded. "I see that." Matt didn't, but Wyatt couldn't deny her affection and almost fanatic protectiveness of her brother. Matt was lucky to have family who cared about him. "You would do anything to protect him."

She nodded. "Of course I would."

"Then give him some space," Wyatt suggested. "Don't lecture and antagonize him. You'll just make him more determined."

She tilted her head as if considering his advice. But, despite her cautious nature, she was driven—so driven that she worked Saturdays in an office where no one else worked the weekend. He suspected she was incapable of doing nothing.

She confirmed that suspicion when she asked him, "So what do I do?"

"Me." He only said it to tease her—because he liked the flash of anger in her green eyes. But to himself he could admit that he wasn't entirely joking.

Fortunately for him she was too cautious and uptight to take his suggestion. She was exactly the type of woman he wouldn't risk getting involved with—she was manipulative and controlling and had no respect for his career. Hell, being a Hotshot wasn't just a career to him; it was as much his identity as his name.

He was glad that Fiona considered him too great a risk for her. Because she was too great a risk for him…

6

WYATT WAS RIGHT. She would do anything to protect her brother. Even him…

But if she was going to start something with Wyatt—and she was afraid it had already started—then she owed it to Howard to officially end it with him first.

Whatever *it* was…

Friday night dinner. An occasional after-dinner romp between the sheets. But those romps had never made her feel like Wyatt Andrews's kisses had. She had never wanted Howard the way she wanted Wyatt.

What was wrong with her?

Howard was stable and safe. He was good-looking, too, in that sexy nerd kind of way she'd always found most attractive. She'd always preferred brain over brawn…until now.

Until Wyatt.

But then, he wasn't just brawn. There was more to him than she'd realized. He had a psychology degree. Was he messing with her? Manipulating her?

Maybe. For Matthew, it was a risk she was willing

to take. Because Wyatt was right. She couldn't get through to her brother. He would never listen to her.

But he would listen to Wyatt. She just had to get Wyatt to tell her brother what she wanted him to hear. And he'd suggested the way she could get him to do that. By doing him... If not for that kiss, she might have thought he'd been joking. He had a warped sense of humor—warped toward naughtiness. But the way he'd kissed her...

She shivered at just the thought of his mouth moving over hers. What if she actually made love with him...

She shook her head, trying to get the image from her mind. It wouldn't come to that. She wouldn't let it. But it had already gone too far.

She pulled her car to the curb beside Howard's house. Dread filled her. He had been so disappointed the night before when she'd forgotten their date. She hoped he wouldn't be too upset over her ending their relationship.

She didn't want to hurt him. He deserved better, though. He deserved a woman who wanted him the way she wanted Wyatt Andrews. She drew in a breath and braced herself to open the car door and confront him. But she'd only reached for the handle when she saw him.

Howard strode toward the front door of his tidy brick Colonial. But he wasn't alone. His arm was wound tightly around the slender shoulders of the blonde woman at his side. He stopped at the door, but instead of opening it, he pulled the blonde up against him. His hands slid over her ass, pressing her into his hips. And he kissed her.

The woman linked her arms around his neck and kissed him back with passion and familiarity.

Fiona wasn't jealous, but her mercurial temper ignited. She didn't remember opening the car door. But she was suddenly standing on the sidewalk right in front of them. She cleared her throat of her anger and disgust. "Excuse me…"

Howard jumped and stumbled back from the woman. "What the hell—"

"Exactly," Fiona said. "What the hell?"

"Who are you?" the woman asked.

And suddenly everything made sense. There was a reason she only saw Howard one night a week and it had nothing to do with his being too busy or her being too busy. It was the way he'd wanted it. It was the reason he hadn't been able to reschedule their missed date to another night.

She held out her hand toward the blonde. "I'm Friday night. I'm assuming you're Saturday?"

"Fiona," Howard said, his voice sharp with disapproval and panic.

The woman's eyes widened with sudden realization. "He sees you on Fridays?"

Fiona shook her head. "Not anymore. Maybe you can get both nights." She turned away and headed back down the sidewalk toward her vehicle. That had been a hell of lot easier than she'd imagined. She should have been relieved. But she was still pissed.

At herself more than at him. She'd been a fool. Why hadn't she ever questioned why he'd had so little time for her? Maybe because she hadn't wanted more with him.

"Fiona," he said. "Don't go…"

She was already gone.

And apparently the blonde was leaving, too, because he called out, "Brenda, don't go!"

Fiona swallowed a chuckle, more amused than angry now. Unfortunately, he probably had a Thursday and Sunday afternoon, too. So he wouldn't be alone for long.

But then, maybe neither would she…

WYATT STEPPED INTO the Northern Lakes Fire Station and headed, feet dragging with reluctance, toward Braden's office. After last night he'd be lucky if he still had a job. But he couldn't avoid his boss any longer. He rapped his knuckles against the open door, as he had at Fiona's office, and stepped inside. While Fiona's office had been refined and elegant, Braden's desk was heavy, dinged up and metal, which was rusting slightly. And the walls were cement blocks painted almost the gray of their original color.

"I checked the campsites in the national forest," he said. "No sign of any fires…" Just like when Dawson had checked the night before. But he refrained from reminding his boss of that.

"Yet," Braden murmured. "No signs yet."

"Maybe it wasn't a fire your sixth sense was warning you about," Wyatt suggested. "Maybe it was last night…"

Braden glanced up and glared at him. But then his gaze focused on the bruise on Wyatt's face and he chuckled.

"You don't look much better," Wyatt said. But maybe he shouldn't have reminded him of the scratches on his arms and his neck from where the women had tried to tear off his T-shirt.

Too late. Braden winced and touched one of the angrier-looking gouges in his skin. "Yeah, going to that club—that was a great idea."

"Not one of my better suggestions," Wyatt admitted.

"You did it to check up on her."

"Who?"

"Your friend's sister," Braden said, then wistfully added, "Fiona…"

Just the sound of her name had desire punching him like a blow to the gut.

"I didn't know she'd be there."

"Then it was just luck that we showed up when we did," Braden skeptically remarked. "You rescued her from that guy at the bar."

"Hey, don't be jealous," Wyatt teased. "I rescued you from those drunk women on the dance floor."

Braden touched his scratches and winced again. "You took your time."

"I couldn't tell if you were enjoying it or not," Wyatt admitted.

Braden glared at him.

"Hey, women were literally ripping off your clothes—what's not to enjoy?"

The glare got sharper and more pointed.

Wyatt touched his chest, checking for a hole—because his boss was nearly boring one through him with that angry stare. "I already admitted it wasn't my best idea."

"Is Fiona?" Braden asked.

His heart started pounding harder and faster at just the sound of her name. "Is Fiona what?" But he knew…

"Your best idea?"

He couldn't deny that he was attracted to her. Because he was, generally, an honest man, he shook his head. "No, she's not."

"You're ignoring your own advice?"

"I probably would," he admitted, "if the lady was interested. But she's not."

Braden's mouth curved into a mocking grin.

"Yeah, yeah, I know," Wyatt said. "I must be losing my mojo, huh? She's not interested, and you're the one whose clothes women are tearing off." Acting befuddled and disappointed, he scratched his head. Well, he wasn't actually *acting* disappointed. He was. About Fiona…

Not the women ripping off his clothes. He glanced at Braden's scratches and shook his head again.

The captain pointed toward the doorway behind Wyatt. "I think someone's looking for you…"

He heard the heels first, clicking against the cement floor. Braden must have heard them, too. Maybe the captain's sense of hearing was as acute as his sixth sense about fires. Along with the click of her heels, there was the electronic beep of a cell phone announcing either a text, email or voice mail.

At least, his beeped for all of those messages. But it had been curiously quiet lately. He'd been harassing Braden to get back out there, but now Wyatt realized how long it had been since *he'd* dated anyone—or even hooked up with anyone.

Maybe that was why he was so attracted to Fiona O'Brien. He'd just been suffering from female deprivation.

"You don't know it's her," Wyatt said. He had made

a false assumption the last time she'd come to the station, mistaking her for Braden returning to the workout room. But his quickening pulse told him that it was her—even before she came around the corner, the fluorescent lights making her red hair shimmer.

She didn't see him; instead she was focused on her phone, probably reading a text. Whatever it said had that glint of anger flashing in her green eyes.

"What has Matt done now?" he asked.

"Matt?" Braden asked.

She slid her phone into her briefcase-style purse and looked up—at his boss instead of him. "Matthew Hamilton. He's my brother. Don't you know him? He applied to be a firefighter."

Braden shot a significant glance at Wyatt. He recognized the name; he never forgot the name of an applicant.

Wyatt answered for him, "The captain can't discuss candidates with anyone."

She looked at him, then back at Braden, who nodded his head in confirmation. He couldn't discuss candidates with anyone outside the team. Hell, he couldn't even discuss the process with Wyatt since he wasn't on the hiring committee. The application process had to be wrapping up soon, though. All decisions were usually made—rejection letters sent—before wildfire season officially began. So if Matt was going to become a firefighter, he probably would have received interview callbacks already. And if he had, he would have shared that news with Wyatt.

Wyatt should have explained to Fiona that she had nothing to worry about with her brother. But then she would have no reason to keep seeking him out.

And he liked that she'd come to see him again.

From inside her bag, her phone beeped again.

She glared at her purse as if it was responsible for the beeping.

"That's not Matt," Wyatt surmised. She wouldn't be so irritated with her brother contacting her. He'd seen how much she loved him.

"It's nothing," she murmured. Forcing a smile, she focused on Braden again. At least he hoped she was forcing that smile, because it was entirely too bright, too beautiful, to be wasted on Braden. But then, she was apparently only flirting, because she nearly batted her lashes as she coyly asked, "You really can't talk about my brother's application?"

The captain's eyes wide with appreciation for her beauty, he shook his head regretfully.

And that annoying twinge of jealousy struck Wyatt again.

Then Braden added, "Legally we can't discuss applicants with anyone not involved in the hiring process." He gave Wyatt a pointed stare—probably to remind him that he wasn't involved in that process and had no business discussing an applicant with anyone for any reason.

"I should be involved," Fiona said. "No one knows my brother better than I do."

Wyatt knew the kid better than she did. Far better. He knew how strained their relationship was. And if she persisted, she was only going to strain it more—maybe to the breaking point.

He slid his hand around Fiona's arm and turned her around. "You're not going to harass the captain about Matt."

"I wouldn't—"

"It's my job to protect the other members of my team," Wyatt said.

Braden snorted and murmured, "You didn't do that great a job last night…"

Ignoring his boss, Wyatt continued steering Fiona down the hall toward the exit.

She wriggled her arm free of his grasp. "Are you throwing me out?"

"I'm walking you out," he said. "I'm a gentleman."

She snorted now. "Yeah, right. Just earlier today you told me to sleep with you to take my brother out of the running for a Hotshot position."

He was glad they'd stepped outside the door so Braden wouldn't have overheard. Although, given the captain's hearing, he might have. He hadn't missed the sound of her heels at all. "I didn't tell you that. There's nothing you can do about Matt's application."

There was nothing she needed to do because Matt wasn't going to qualify to become a firefighter, let alone a Hotshot. Wyatt had become his mentor for a reason—because the kid had gotten into trouble, and even though it had been as a juvenile, his record wasn't sealed, and the felony automatically disqualified him as an applicant. Because he'd been Matt's court-appointed mentor, Wyatt couldn't tell Fiona about the trouble her brother had been in, though. And Braden had just reminded him that he couldn't discuss the applicants with anyone. Wyatt might not get fired for crossing the line, but he didn't want to put the team in jeopardy, either. If Matt thought they'd discussed him and sued…

"Then why did you tell me to *do* you?"

He chuckled. "I was kidding." But that wasn't entirely truthful.

He followed her toward her car—which was parked in the lot next to the department pickup.

"It was just a suggestion," he said. "More of an offer…"

Her phone beeped again. Maybe it was another guy trying to get her attention. But she was here, with him.

"Is that why you came to see me?" he asked. "You decided to take me up on my offer?"

She glared at him—or maybe she was glaring at that phone. She grabbed it from her bag and pushed a button on the side of it. Before the screen went black as it powered off, he saw one of her texts.

"'We never said we were exclusive,'" he read over her shoulder. "Ouch…"

"Excuse me," she said, her face flushing either with anger over his presumptuousness or embarrassment at his finding out what had happened.

"Some dick cheated on you?"

"Howard," she said his name bitterly.

"A Howard cheats?" he asked. "Sounds like an accountant…"

Her blush darkened to nearly the color of her hair. "He is an accountant."

He laughed now. "An accountant cheats? Do the statistics support that conclusion?"

"My statistics are for mortality rates," she clarified. "Not cheating."

He reached out and fingered a strand of her fiery hair. "With your temper, I think cheating on you probably would lead to mortality."

She shook her head and, inadvertently or maybe intentionally, tugged her hair free from his grasp. "He's not worth prison time."

"He's not worth your time," Wyatt readily agreed. "You probably figured him for a better risk, didn't you?"

She sighed. "He's right, though. We never said we were exclusive. I just assumed..."

Wyatt cursed. "Don't make excuses for him. The guy's an idiot. He had you—he shouldn't have been seeing other women, too."

She tilted her head and stared up at him.

"What?"

"I'm surprised you feel that way," she said. "I didn't figure you would be a proponent of exclusivity."

"I'm not a proponent of *commitment*," he clarified.

"What's the difference?" she asked.

"Commitment is promising love, marriage and forever," he said. And he couldn't restrain the shudder that rippled through his body. "I can't make a promise like that..."

She nodded. "Of course not. Why would you make a promise you wouldn't be able to keep?"

"Why do you think I wouldn't?"

"A man like you—a Hotshot—can't promise anyone forever."

"Not and also keep his job," Wyatt murmured in agreement. "But exclusivity and commitment are different. While I won't promise anyone forever, I will promise that while I'm sleeping—" he leaned closer, pressing his chest against her breasts "—with you, you're the only one I'm sleeping with."

"I'm not sleeping with you," she said.

He allowed his disappointment to show. "And I

thought that's why you tracked me down at the firehouse. Again."

She shook her head. "I just wanted to talk about…" She glanced down at her phone, as if she expected it to ring even though she'd shut it off.

"Matt?" he prodded her. He suspected Howard was the one on her mind right now, though.

She nodded.

"Then come back to my place," he suggested. "And we can talk."

She stared up at him as if considering it.

He expected another rejection, so he was surprised when she nodded.

"I'll show you where it is," he offered. And he walked around to her passenger's side. When she clicked the locks, he slid into the car next to her.

Her hand shook slightly as she reached for the ignition. "We're just going to talk."

"Sure," he said. "But it's okay if you want to use me to get back at Howard. I'll make the supreme sacrifice— my body for your vengeance."

He expected her to laugh or slap him. But she said nothing. Was she actually considering it?

7

"WHAT DID YOU EXPECT? Mirrors on the ceiling and black satin everywhere?"

Wyatt's question drew Fiona's attention away from her survey of his home. She knew she'd been openly staring because she was shocked.

"Or a gun rack and animal heads on the walls?"

She laughed. "Maybe. I expected it to be more than a block away from the fire station. Why did you have to ride with me?" She'd thought her car was big until he'd ridden in the passenger's seat, his shoulder rubbing against hers over the console.

"I wanted to make sure you didn't get lost."

"It's not like it's out in the wilderness," she said— which was what she'd expected. She hadn't expected the little yellow bungalow behind the white picket fence. The walls inside were yellow and white, too. Yellow plaster and white bead board. "You're a forest ranger. Aren't you supposed to live in the forest?"

He chuckled. "I'm not Smokey Bear. I am a forest ranger, but this town is actually part of the national forest. So I'm assigned to this area as a firefighter."

"But you travel all over…" That was part of what Matthew had said he found so exciting about the job. The travel. And the danger…

The women, too.

Fiona hadn't realized there were firefighter groupies—until she'd seen the women go after the stripper dressed as a firefighter.

He nodded. "When the Hotshot team gets called in, I go—wherever we're called, wherever we're needed."

And it was that simple to him, putting his life at risk. He was called and he went.

Panic at the thought—at the potential loss—had pressure settling heavily on her chest. "I shouldn't have come here," she murmured. It had been a mistake.

"Why did you?" he asked. "To get back at ol' Howard?" He wriggled his dark brows above blue eyes that glittered with amusement.

Was the man ever serious about anything? Or was he just a tease?

She was tempted to call his bluff—to see if he would actually let her use him, or if he would back down if she acted interested. Wyatt Andrews might not be the playboy she'd thought he was.

As he'd already pointed out, there were no mirrors on his ceilings, and from what she could see of his bedroom through the open door, no black satin, either. A flannel quilt covered the mattress instead.

"I came here because I wanted to talk to you about Matthew," she said.

"We talked this morning," he reminded her. "I gave you my advice." He had been careful to keep that to her relationship with her brother and not his actual application, though.

"I want more than your advice," she admitted.

He wriggled his brows again and stepped closer to her. "What do you want, Fiona?"

Him.

She wanted him—and not to get back at Howard. If not for his incessant texts, she wouldn't have given the accountant another thought. Sure, he was a jerk. But only her pride was a little wounded that she hadn't been enough to keep him satisfied.

Maybe it was that wounded pride that had her lifting her hand to Wyatt's chest. Instead of pushing him away, she stroked her fingers over the soft material of his black Forest Service Fire Department T-shirt. She could feel his muscles rippling and his heart beating beneath her fingertips.

"Fiona…"

"Help me," she implored him. "Help me convince Matthew that he's not cut out to be a firefighter, let alone a Hotshot."

He shook his head. "I can't talk to him about this. But you don't need to worry about him. It's—"

She pressed her fingers over his lips. She didn't want to hear it—whatever protest or excuse he might give her—like his delusion that what he did wasn't overly dangerous. She had the statistics, so many statistics, to prove him wrong. But he'd already made it clear that he considered her stats a joke. He'd also made it clear that he wasn't going to help her with Matthew.

But maybe she could change his mind.

So she slid one hand around the nape of his neck, tugged his head down and replaced her fingers with her lips. She pressed her mouth to his and kissed him. But his lips remained in a tight line. He didn't kiss her back; his mouth didn't move at all. And she felt the tension in his neck.

Tammy was wrong. Fiona wouldn't be able to sway Wyatt with sex. She couldn't even tempt him. He had obviously just been teasing her. He didn't actually find her attractive—at least not attractive enough to want her.

GOD, HE WANTED HER. But Wyatt knew what she was up to—what she was willing to sacrifice to protect her brother. Matt wouldn't appreciate her interference. And it was unnecessary anyway. Her brother wouldn't get on to the team. But he couldn't share that with her without risking a lawsuit against the department.

He had no business telling her anything. But he understood how much she loved her brother—so much that she was willing to sleep with Wyatt. His hands shaking a little, he grasped her shoulders and held her back. His muscles contracted; he wanted to pull her closer—wanted to hold her against him.

Not away…

"So you're all talk," she murmured with a sigh that almost sounded disappointed. If the blush on her skin meant anything, she was also embarrassed.

Or aroused.

But he hadn't touched her. He hadn't kissed her back. He wanted to…

Oh, God, how he wanted to.

"But when I call your bluff…"

"Is that what you're doing?" he asked. "Just calling my bluff? Seeing if I'm all talk?" She could be messing with him. For as much as he'd messed with her, he deserved it.

"Are you?" she asked. Despite his hands on her shoulders, she leaned in—pushing her breasts against his chest. "You've been flirting with me. Kissing me…"

He couldn't deny it. So he nodded and admitted, "That I have." He leaned down, close enough that his nose nearly touched hers, and he added, "But then I like playing with fire."

She sucked in a breath. It was his breath—he was that close, his lips nearly touching hers. He could feel the heat—the softness…

But he denied them both that contact.

"And we would create a firestorm," he said, "we would burn up the sheets."

"Wyatt…" she murmured. And she reached for him again, her fingers sliding into the hair at his nape.

"But you don't like playing with fire," he reminded her.

Her brow furrowed slightly. "I don't…" she said softly. "I don't want to get burned."

He was afraid that he was the one who might get burned. And he was usually so careful. He had never brought a woman like her home before—one who openly disapproved of his job, who had already called it too risky.

A woman like her would give him ultimatums, would make him give up the job he loved more than anything else. He needed to let her go. Hell, he needed to throw her out the door and hope that she forgot where he lived.

But his hands still clasped her shoulders. He couldn't let her go, let alone throw her out. But maybe he'd said enough. Maybe he'd scared her into remembering why she wanted nothing to do with him.

He was too great a risk.

But her hands tugged his head down again, closing that small space between their mouths. Her lips met his, moving like warm silk across his own. He didn't resist. He couldn't.

His control snapped and he kissed her back with all the passion burning inside him. He parted her lips and dipped his tongue inside, sliding it over hers.

She was so damn hot. Her mouth wasn't enough. He needed more. He needed to be inside her body. He picked her up.

She gasped in surprise. And maybe fear. He tensed, struggling for control over himself. His voice gruff with desire, he asked, "Who's bluffing now?"

8

FIONA'S PULSE RACED with fear—and desire. Her legs dangled over the arm beneath them; his other arm wrapped around her back. He held her easily, as if she weighed nothing. And maybe to Wyatt, who lifted weights regularly, she didn't weigh much. She could feel the muscles in his arms, hard and bulging.

"Were you just bluffing, Fiona?" he asked her.

She was used to his wicked grin, to the amusement dancing in his blue eyes. But he was serious now. Tense. A muscle twitched beneath the stubble on his tightly clenched jaw.

He was right. She didn't play with fire. She was afraid of getting burned. So she should have wriggled free of his grasp and run for the door.

Instead she wrapped her arm around his neck and clung to him, pressing her lips to his jaw. "No…"

"Are you sure?" he asked.

She hadn't sounded it. She had sounded tentative and scared even to her own ears. And she was scared.

But she wasn't going to back out now. She told herself that it was because of Matthew. Because she would do anything to stop him from making a mistake.

But who was going to stop Fiona?

Not her.

She kissed him again, this time on the lips. She slipped her tongue out, just the tip, and traced his mouth.

He groaned and deepened the kiss.

She felt the thrust of his tongue and tasted his passion. And her head grew light as he carried her. With his long strides, he only took a few steps to cross the living room and pass through the open bedroom door.

He laid her down on the flannel quilt. And she was glad. If he'd put her on her feet, her legs might have buckled. They trembled. She trembled all over. She'd never felt that way before—so nervous and excited and aroused.

And he'd barely touched her. He'd only kissed her.

But he touched her now. Lightly. His hands trailed down her sides, tracing the indent of her waist, the curve of her hips and down along her thighs and legs. He tugged off her shoes. The heels dropped with loud clunks onto his hardwood floor.

The sound startled her into sitting up. Maybe it should have brought her to her senses. But he kissed her again with such passion and possession that she wanted more.

She needed more.

She helped him undress her, shrugging out of her jacket and tugging her sweater over her head. The pins in her bun caught in the wool and pulled free of her hair. It tumbled down around shoulders that were bare but for the thin straps of her lacy bra.

He groaned, the sound almost tortured. He stared

at her so intensely that she felt his gaze like a caress, sliding over the slopes of her breasts. "You are so damn beautiful…"

She knew she was pretty. While she had her father's coloring, she had her mom's delicate features—the face that had attracted men like Wyatt, men who craved danger and excitement.

And for a moment, she worried that she would disappoint him. She must not have been enough for Howard. Maybe those doubts played across her face because he cursed.

She glanced up at him.

His voice thick with desire, he murmured, "The accountant was a jackass."

She had never wanted Howard the way she did Wyatt. She reached for him, pushing his coat from his shoulders—his broad, strong shoulders. Her hands ran over them in a light caress.

And he shuddered.

Even before she took off his T-shirt. Her fingers teased up his washboard abs and over his chest as she rolled up the soft fabric before pulling it over his head.

"Damn, woman," he said. "And you called me a tease…"

"I called you a flirt," she corrected him. "And I'm not a tease…"

If she was, she would have kept it to kissing. She would have just implied she'd make love with him if he helped her with Matthew. But she wasn't a tease.

She was probably a fool, though.

But then his hands were there, easily undoing the clasp at the back of her bra. A chill raced over her skin as she acknowledged his expertise. He'd had a lot of women before her. He would have a lot more after her.

Despite his talk of exclusivity, she knew and accepted that this night was probably all she would have with him. A one-night stand.

She hadn't had one—at least that she'd realized before making love with the man. This time she knew. And maybe there was comfort in that—that this wasn't serious.

Her heart wasn't at risk. She wasn't going to fall for Wyatt Andrews. She was only going to sleep with him.

She reached for the buckle of his belt. But his hands covered hers.

"Not so fast," he said.

And he pushed her back onto the bed again. His fingers found the side zipper of her skirt and tugged it down, and then he tugged down the skirt, too. So she lay on his flannel quilt in only her lace panties. But he quickly disposed of those, as well.

He groaned again as first his gaze caressed her. Then his hands followed the path his eyes had. "Fiona..."

She touched him, too. She skimmed her palms over his chest and shoulders and arms. All those muscles rippled...

But she wanted more.

His mouth replaced his hands, his lips trailing down her neck and over her collarbone. She shifted on the bed as tension began to wind inside her. His mouth continued up the slope of her breast until his lips closed around a nipple.

She moaned as sensations raced through her. Her skin heated and her heart pounded. She ran her fingers through his hair. She'd once thought it too long. But she loved the softness of it, loved tangling her fingers in the silky black strands.

Then she clutched at his shoulders as he continued to tease her, tugging at that nipple, nipping it gently with his teeth. She nearly came.

"You are a tease," she accused him. And she reached between them and found his belt again. He didn't stop her this time as she undid the buckle and the button of his jeans. Metal sighed as she lowered the zipper. Then she sighed as, even bound in his boxers, his erection sprang into her hand.

He groaned. Then he was kissing her again—deeply. His tongue thrust inside her mouth the way she needed his cock inside her body. She needed him.

She pushed down his boxers and wrapped her hand around the silky thickness. It was every bit as impressive as the rest of him. "Wyatt…"

But he pulled back. Maybe he needed to find a condom.

He didn't reach for one, though. Instead, he slid down her body, his lips whispering along the valley between her breasts, across her stomach and over her hips until he settled between her legs.

"Wyatt…"

He teased her with just the tip of his tongue against her clit, flicking back and forth. She whimpered as sensations raced through her. Her skin heated, and her pulse quickened, her heart pounding so hard she could feel it beating in her breast. She had never felt so much…need. He was driving her crazy!

He continued to tease her with his tongue. And with his touch. His hands moved over her body, caressing her naked skin. He cupped her breasts and teased her nipples with his thumbs.

The tension built, winding so tightly that she felt as if she might snap in two. She arched her back, and he gently squeezed her breasts. She needed him. She reached down, intending to tug him up—but her hands clenched his shoulders instead.

Then his tongue slid inside her.

And, her nails digging into his skin, she came—screaming his name. He didn't let up. He slipped two fingers inside her while his tongue went back to flicking over her clit. Before her pleasure even ebbed, the tension built again. She couldn't catch her breath. She couldn't slow the pounding of her heart. She had never felt like this—had never felt this much this quickly. Usually it took a while for her to find release. But her panting became a low keening moan as she came again.

Finally he moved back.

And she expected to find him chuckling over how easily he'd aroused her. How quickly he'd satisfied her.

But there was no humor in his eyes—only intense desire. He slipped off his underwear and rolled on the condom he'd found. It had to be extra long—like he was. Her heart began to pound even more frantically. Then he was there—between her legs. He planted his palms next to her head, his arms bulging as they supported his weight. And he leaned forward. As his mouth lowered and covered hers, his body lowered, too. And she felt him there, his hips against hers, as his erection rubbed against her clit.

His lips parted hers as the kiss grew in heat and intensity. She could taste her own passion, taste how much he'd already pleased her. His tongue slid inside her mouth—deeply. He moved one hand and reached between them. The tip of his erection stroked her clit again, and she moaned in anticipation, wanting more—wanting him.

She spread her legs wider and arched, and finally he thrust inside her—gently at first, just teasing her. She clutched at his shoulders then ran her hands down his back to his butt. It was as tightly muscled as the rest of his gorgeously masculine body. She grasped his butt, pulling his hips toward her. So he thrust again, harder.

He was so big—so thick and long—that he filled her and then some. She arched her hips again, trying to take him deeper—trying to take all of him.

"You are so damn hot," he murmured as he kissed her again.

He brushed her tongue with his, kissing her deeply as he entered her over and over. The tension was building in her again…

Finally breaking the kiss, he lifted her legs so that she took him deeper still. And he thrust—hard and fast.

She clung to him, her arms locked around his back. And she matched each move—until her body tensed and then shattered. This orgasm rocked her, curling her toes and making her scream as she came and came.

A few moments later he tensed and a groan ripped from his throat. Before she could find her breath again, he pulled up and rolled off the bed. Her legs would have folded beneath her if she'd tried to walk away—as he was walking away. Her body trembled in the aftermath of the intense pleasure he'd given her. But he wasn't even fazed.

Was that how he was? He got what he wanted and would then throw her out?

Through the open door off the master bedroom, she heard water running. Was he already showering her off his body?

Embarrassment rushed through her, heating her skin. But before she could recover enough to scramble for her clothes, he was back. He lifted her.

Maybe he intended to throw her out—as she was—naked.

But while he held her in one arm, he jerked back the quilt with the other. Then he laid down and covered them both with it, his strong arms bulging with muscles wrapped around her. "Give me a few minutes," he said.

"Few minutes…"

To show her out?

He nodded, his chin bumping against the top of her head. "And we'll do it again…"

Her heart rate, which had just begun to slow, raced again. Do it again? Would she survive another time? She couldn't risk it.

First his breathing slowed from the panting that had matched hers moments ago. His chest rose and fell softly beneath her head. He'd fallen asleep.

She could have been insulted. Or irritated. Instead she was just relieved. She waited a few moments longer—not because it felt so wonderful, so perfect snuggling against his hard, hot body. She waited to make sure that he wouldn't easily awaken. Then she slipped from beneath his arm and beneath that quilt. She quietly and quickly grabbed her clothes and shoes and carried them into the living room, where she dressed faster than she ever had. She found her purse and ran out of there as if she was the one going to a fire.

But she wasn't going to a fire. She was running from one.

WYATT COULDN'T HAVE been asleep long. He was used to the power nap—the quick ten or fifteen minutes that was sometimes all he could manage when working a fire. If it was a big one, the team wasn't able to sleep sometimes for days. Maybe even a week without more than brief power naps in a safe zone.

It was all he needed to be alert and ready to go.

His body was alert, his cock hard and ready to go— aching to go. He had to thrust inside her again—had to see if she'd really felt as hot and incredible as he'd thought she had.

But maybe it had all just been a dream. Because she was gone…

She'd left behind only the heat of her body and the sweet, musky scent of sex.

Had she regretted what they'd done? Was that why she'd left so quickly? Or maybe she had only wanted revenge against Howard and she'd gone off to rub it in the accountant's face that she'd taken another lover, too.

Or had he only been a one-night stand?

He waited for the relief. It was good that she'd taken off. He couldn't afford to get used to her being in his bed, in his arms. He couldn't afford to get attached to a woman like her.

It was better that she'd just been using him.

The doorbell rang, and a weight he hadn't even realized was there lifted from his chest. Wrapped only in the quilt, he hurried to the door and opened it with a grin.

"Missed me already?"

"I just saw you this morning," Matt Hamilton replied. "But somehow I don't think you're talking to me."

He had to stop doing that—had to stop assuming someone's identity before he saw her or his face.

"No," he admitted.

Matt glanced outside. "Were you expecting my sister?"

The kid was smart. Fiona was right; he needed to stay in college. He should have never dropped out before learning if he'd gotten a job with the Forest Service Fire Department. Wyatt had already said as much to him, but the kid had been certain that he'd get hired. He hadn't heard anything Wyatt had subtly brought up. Maybe he'd been too subtle then.

But he knew Fiona's jackhammer approach wasn't working with her brother, either.

Matt snapped his fingers in front of Wyatt's face. He must have been zoned out. And he asked again, "Were you expecting my sister at your door?"

He had been hoping but he hadn't actually expected her. So he was able to answer honestly, "No."

The kid's brown eyes narrowed with suspicion. "I thought I saw her car here just a little while ago."

She hadn't been gone for long, then. If only he'd awakened a few minutes earlier…

Matt would have caught them together. That wouldn't have been good. The kid was already bristling with anger. But Wyatt didn't know which of them he was angry at, him or Fiona.

"There are a lot of cars like hers," Wyatt pointed out. And there were—since it was a top safety pick, families and old people loved them.

"Not parked outside your house," Matt persisted.

That was true.

"You don't date women who drive cars like hers."

That was true, too. The women he dated didn't care about safety. Theirs or anyone else's.

The realization gave him pause. He had considered that a good thing?

But it was—because those women didn't care how dangerous his job was. They wanted him as he was; they wouldn't try to change him.

"No, I don't date women like your sister," he agreed. So it was good that she'd snuck out while he was sleeping. For his sake as much as Matt's.

But her brother's face was still pinched with tension and suspicion. He had probably known Wyatt long enough to recognize when he was being vague to avoid the truth.

Or maybe not, since he had applied to the fire department despite Wyatt's subtle attempts to discourage him.

Matt released a breath he must have been holding and nodded. "Yeah, you're too smart. You won't let fussy Fiona get to you."

He hoped the kid spoke the truth. He hoped he wouldn't let her get to him.

9

WITH A SOFT SIGH, Fiona kicked off her shoes and curled her legs beneath her on Tammy's velour couch. Her friend's place was as colorful as she was—the couch purple, the pillows orange and the walls yellow. But not a soft, warm yellow like the walls of Wyatt's house. These were the color of a highlighter.

Oddly enough, Fiona felt comfortable there. Maybe it was the wine. She took a big sip from the glass her friend had pressed into her hand the moment she'd stepped into the house.

"So tell me about the firefighter," Tammy said.

The wine caught in Fiona's throat, making her sputter for breath. Covering her mouth, she coughed.

Tammy passed her a napkin. "So he was that good?"

She mopped the wine off her chin. "The red was that dry," she said. "It caught me by surprise." Usually Tammy drank sweet wine—more sangria than merlot.

"I thought that was the kind you liked," Tammy said. "I wanted to get you drunk so you would spill details."

"I don't know what you're talking about." Sure, Tammy had advised her to sleep with Wyatt, but Fiona had given her no reason to think she would actually take that advice.

She couldn't believe that she had. She took another sip of the wine. It was more to her taste than Tammy's.

"When I left the club, the firefighter was chatting you up at the bar."

"Oh, the stripper…"

"They prefer to be called exotic dancers," Tammy corrected her.

"You left with the police officer," Fiona said. Of course, she hadn't realized that until Tammy had texted her later—after she'd already stranded her with the stripper.

Tammy giggled. "I wanted him to frisk me. Maybe even cuff me…"

Fiona laughed at her friend's shamelessness. Personality-wise they couldn't be more different. But they had been friends since they were little kids. Even after Fiona's grandparents had been awarded custody and taken her away from Mandy, Tammy had written to her and called her in Florida. They'd stayed in touch.

And when Fiona had moved back, they'd grown even closer. So close that they had a tendency to over-share. Usually…

But Fiona had been too embarrassed to admit much to her friend. They'd also both been very busy the past week, Fiona at the office and Tammy as a hair dresser at a busy beauty salon. So they'd held off on catching up until the following weekend.

A week following Fiona's night—no, it hadn't even been a night—with Wyatt.

"So did he do a full body search?" Fiona asked.

Tammy laughed—her raucous cackle that ended

with a snort. Fiona passed her the napkin to clean up her spattered wine droplets. "I wish," Tammy murmured. "He wound up being all talk."

Fiona's body heated as she flashed back to the conversation she'd had with Wyatt—to how she'd goaded him with that very accusation. But he hadn't been all talk. There had actually been very little talk.

"So what about the firefighter?" Tammy asked.

"Which one?" Fiona asked. "The stripper or…"

Tammy leaned forward. "Oooh, has there been a development with the other firefighter?"

Feeling oddly defensive, Fiona said, "The real firefighter."

Maybe it was just because the stripper had been a jerk that she didn't appreciate Tammy acting as if he was a real firefighter. He didn't deserve to be compared to the people who actually did the dangerous work of fighting fires.

That guy hadn't even been able to fight Wyatt, let alone a wildfire.

"The one who mentors your brother?" Tammy asked. "You took my advice and worked what your mama gave you?"

Fiona took another long sip of wine.

Tammy leaned farther forward and lightly slapped her leg with the napkin. "Come on—share! I tell you everything!"

Fiona groaned. "Don't I know it."

"Hey, it's not my fault that I usually have more to share," she said. "You usually choose to date boring accountants like Howard."

Fiona groaned louder and with great bitterness repeated, *"Howard…"*

"What did Howard do?"

"Saturday night."

"You went out with him Saturday night?" Tammy asked with surprise. Then she groaned. "Don't tell me it's getting serious with *him*."

"No," Fiona said. "Saturday night is *blonde*. Maybe Thursday night is brunette."

"Howard is a man whore?"

Tammy sounded so horrified that Fiona couldn't help but laugh—maybe a little too hard. How had she not known that there had been nothing boring and safe about Howard? Okay, boring maybe…

After having sex with Wyatt, she knew exactly how boring Howard had been. Hopefully Brenda found him more exciting than Fiona had.

"You don't seem too upset about his cheating," Tammy said.

"Now I have my Friday nights free."

"Ohhh…" Tammy murmured. "It is Friday night. I wondered why you were free."

"Now you know."

Her friend tilted her head and studied Fiona through narrowed brown eyes. "I think you're leaving out a lot. What about this real firefighter? He hasn't booked your Friday nights?"

A pang struck Fiona's heart. "No…"

Now Tammy leaned across and sympathetically squeezed her leg. "What's wrong?"

"I took your advice," Fiona admitted.

Tammy smiled. "That's great. So you teased him into helping you with Matt?"

The pang intensified, and Fiona shook her head. "It didn't work."

"Just because he's a real firefighter doesn't mean he's into women," Tammy said. "I wouldn't take it personally that he wasn't interested in your goodies."

Fiona's face heated with embarrassment. "I didn't say that he wasn't interested."

Tammy clapped her hands together. "Oh, you gave up your goodies."

Fiona lifted her glass and drained it.

"Was it that bad?"

She'd thought it was amazing. "He must have thought so. I haven't heard from him since Saturday." Of course, she had run out on him. Maybe he thought she didn't want him to contact her. But she couldn't imagine that stopping Wyatt—if he'd really wanted to see her again, if he'd wanted to be with her again…

"Oh, that's past the three-day waiting period." Tammy patted her leg now with even more sympathy. Probably more like pity.

"And Matthew is as determined as ever to become a Hotshot," Fiona said. "So it was pointless."

"Was it?" Tammy asked, her eyes wide with curiosity. "You didn't answer my question—was it bad?"

Fiona sighed—lust slipping in with the wistfulness.

And Tammy clapped again. "Oh, it was that good."

"Apparently, I am not a good judge of sexual satisfaction," Fiona said. While she'd been completely satisfied—blown away even—he must have been unaffected. "He hasn't called me. And he hasn't talked to Matthew about going back to college." But Matthew wasn't the only one she wanted him to talk to; she wanted to hear from him again, too. Or see him… the way she'd seen him that day—gloriously naked.

Tammy leaned back and sipped her wine, and her brow furrowed as she thought.

Unease chilled Fiona more than Tammy usually chilled her wine. "I don't like that look..."

"Apparently neither did the police officer," Tammy remarked. But she harbored no bitterness. Tammy enjoyed men, but she had never gotten attached to any particular one.

Neither had Fiona. She wasn't upset about Howard. She was actually more upset about Wyatt not calling than her boyfriend cheating. But that was only because the plan hadn't worked. Wyatt hadn't helped her with Matthew.

That was the only reason she'd slept with him.

Liar.

But it didn't matter. It was over now. Her plan hadn't worked.

Tammy leaned forward again and excitement sparkled in her brown eyes. "You have to step up your game, girlfriend."

"What?"

"You probably got rusty with boring Howard. You need to seduce the firefighter."

"I already slept with him."

Tammy waved a hand dismissively. "That was just the awkward first time—not knowing how to tilt your head, being too tense and nervous to let yourself enjoy it."

Heat rushed over Fiona, but it wasn't embarrassment. It was passion as she remembered how much she had enjoyed herself. "I wasn't nervous."

Tammy sighed. "Oh, he was. That was the policeman's problem. He got so nervous that he couldn't perform."

"Wyatt wasn't nervous, either," Fiona said. "He was…" She swallowed hard and wished she hadn't already finished her wine.

"Better than average?"

"Amazing…"

"Then you have to seduce him," Tammy said again. "You might not have been nervous, but I take it you weren't planning to sleep with him."

Fiona shook her head. "No, I wasn't. I just wanted to talk to him—to get him to talk to Matthew for me. But I had just found out about the Howard thing. And…"

She had no excuse. She'd wanted Wyatt. She'd even goaded him into sleeping with her.

"So be ready this time," Tammy said. "Make him fall for you."

"Love?" she asked. She didn't want him to fall for her.

Tammy snorted. "Not love. Lust. Make him fall into lust with you."

Maybe Fiona had had just enough wine that what Tammy said actually made sense. She was going to seduce Wyatt Andrews.

THE ECHO OF rubber striking asphalt followed Wyatt as his feet pounded the road. The impact radiated through his body, but it did nothing to ease the tension. That radiated through his body, too, starting from his groin.

Every time he thought of her…

He grunted as his cock hardened again. It seemed as if he'd had a permanent erection since the night they'd had sex. If only she hadn't snuck out…

If she'd stayed and waited for him to recover, they could have done it again. And again…

Maybe then the tension wouldn't have returned to his body—even more intense than before he'd been with her. Now he knew the release he could find with her—*in* her.

He groaned now and slowed his pace. He could barely walk, let alone run. Fortunately, he was nearing his house. Then he noticed the car parked at the curb and his pace quickened. Matt was right; not many women who drove a car like that would come to his house.

It could only be her.

He stopped at the bottom of the steps leading up to the front porch. And he saw her…sitting on the bench next to the door. She wore a coat, which was understandable given that it was just spring and still kind of cold.

He hadn't noticed it during his jog, though. His body had been too hot—and hard.

He got hotter and harder now—because he suspected all she wore was the coat. She'd crossed her legs, and her jacket had parted over her thighs. She wasn't wearing one of her tight little skirts beneath it.

Her legs were bare as far up as he could see. A high heel dangled from her small foot as her leg moved back and forth—probably to keep her warm.

"You must be freezing," he said.

She shook her head but shivered as a gust of wind blew through the porch railing. It parted her coat farther, and he caught a glimpse of the lace between her legs.

He groaned. "What are you up to, woman?"

Her eyes—those beautiful green eyes—widened with feigned innocence. As if she had no idea what he was talking about.

"And don't tell me that you're here to talk." He'd expected her to come back—to keep trying to get him to talk to Matt for her. But she'd stayed away a week.

And he'd felt too guilty to call her.

If only he could tell her the truth...

That she didn't have to worry about her brother making the Hotshots team or even the Forest Service Fire Department. But Matt shouldn't find out from her, and she wouldn't be able to hide the truth from her brother.

Maybe he could ask Braden when the letters were going out. But his boss had cautioned him every day that week to not discuss any of the applicants with anyone.

Most especially not Fiona.

That was another reason he hadn't called her. Because he wasn't sure he could keep anything from her...

"I'm not here to talk," Fiona replied as she stood. The heels brought her to his chin, so he could easily see down the front of her coat—see that she wore nothing beneath it but a bra with very small cups. Her breasts spilled over them—all creamy cleavage.

He groaned. "Are you trying to seduce me?"

"I'm just trying to get warm," she murmured as she leaned in closer.

Despite the cool air, he was sweaty from his run. So he stepped back and pushed open the door. "It was unlocked. You should have let yourself in."

"I wasn't sure I was welcome," she said, and her smile slipped.

His not calling had hurt her feelings. Given what had happened with the idiot accountant, he shouldn't have been so insensitive.

"You're welcome anytime," he assured her. He'd love if one night she would slide back into his bed as she'd slid out of it, slipping between the sheets and into his arms.

She stepped inside and he followed, closing the door behind them. "Do you want to take my coat?" she asked, as she loosened the belt and it slipped off one bare shoulder.

"You're definitely trying to seduce me."

"Is it working?" she asked.

"You know that it is…" His shorts were loose, his reaction apparent in the tent he'd made of the nylon fabric.

Her smile widened, and amusement sparkled in her green eyes. She was playing him. He knew it.

"Fiona," he said. "You don't want me to talk to Matt for you…" Especially not after her brother had seen her car parked outside his house. He would be furious with her for interfering in his life.

Her smile dimmed for a moment with obvious disappointment. That was what she wanted. But she shook her head in denial. "I don't want to talk about my brother. I don't want to talk at all."

She turned around and opened the coat, dropping it to reveal tantalizing bits of red lace. The woman was red-hot. And Wyatt had never been able to stay away from the heat. She was the one who'd started this game—of playing with fire. She was trying to manipulate him, just as he'd worried she would. So maybe she deserved a little payback.

He grabbed her and tossed her over his shoulder. Dangling down his back, she squealed with surprise. His hand covered her ass—her sweet, soft ass—to stop her from wriggling down as he carried her through his bedroom to the bathroom.

He opened the glass door of the shower and carried her inside with him. Keeping her away from the spray, he turned on the faucet. At the initial shock of cold water, he lost his breath on a gasp. But then the water warmed.

So he released her to slide down his front. Impatient that he couldn't feel her, he dragged off his clothes and tossed them over the glass doors.

"What are you doing?" she asked.

"Taking a shower."

"I didn't need to take one, too," she said.

She'd been wearing makeup and had curled her hair. She'd looked beautiful then, but she looked more beautiful now. The water had washed away the mascara and makeup, leaving her face bare. Those scraps of lace were transparent now that they were wet. He discarded them as quickly as he had his clothes.

"Oh, you're dirty," he told her, "showing up at my door dressed like you were—or undressed like you were."

Her annoyance vanished with a smile—it was both seductive and somehow shy, too. That jackass Howard had shaken her confidence a little, and Wyatt probably hadn't helped with not calling her. So he intended to show her just how desirable she was.

He leaned down and kissed her—claiming her with his mouth and his tongue. Her lips moved beneath his, parting on a sigh and then a moan. She let him inside and then she teased him with the tip of her wet little tongue.

He groaned. And his already tortured body tensed more. He had to have her. Now. So with the water sluicing over them, he lifted her again. But this time he didn't throw her over his shoulder. He only held her as high as his waist, so that the end of his cock could nudge between her legs.

Raised as she was, he could reach her breasts with his mouth. He teased each nipple with the tip of his tongue before nipping it lightly with his teeth. She moaned as he continued to tease her—with his mouth and with the tip of his cock rubbing against her clit. Back and forth. Back and forth...

His cock throbbed and pulsed, desperate to plunge inside her. But he held back. He wanted to please her first. He wanted to drive her as crazy as she drove him.

Her hands gripped his shoulders, her nails digging into his skin. Her heart beat hard; he could feel it pounding beneath the silky sleek skin of her breast. She was close. He wanted to push her over the edge.

He tugged her nipple with his teeth, pulling on the already distended point. She arched her back, pushing her nipple farther into his mouth—wriggling in his arms. He tightened his grip on her sweet ass, his hands caressing and squeezing the soft curves. Then he moved his fingers between her legs. He stroked her, back and forth, before plunging two fingers inside.

She cried out with pleasure, and her body trembled in his arms. She was slick when his cock slid inside her. Wet and ready for him.

She wrapped her legs and arms around him, meeting his thrusts. She slid up and down, riding him. The shower filled with steam. He wasn't sure if it was from the heat of the water or her. She was so damn hot. So wet.

Her passion scorched him with its intensity and incited his own. The tension inside him was nearly unbearable. But he held back—wanting to please her so much that she wouldn't slip away as she had last time. When he was done, he wanted her to feel too boneless to move.

The tension had to be building in her, too, because she whimpered and bit her lip. Then she writhed against him. She arched and shifted, taking him deeper with each thrust. And finally she came with a loud cry.

Despite the tension racking him, making his muscles tremble, he held on to his release. And holding on to her, he turned off the faucet and stepped out of the shower. He nearly slipped as his bare feet hit the tiled bathroom floor.

She squealed and clutched at him. But he stayed inside her as he carried her into the bedroom. Then finally he pulled free and laid her on the flannel comforter.

"We're going to get everything all wet," she protested.

"That's the idea," he said. And because he had to taste her, he parted her legs and moved his mouth to her core. He slid his tongue over her clit. Her nails scraped his skin as she clutched at his shoulders.

"Wyatt…"

It wasn't a protest. She was nearly ready to come again. But he only teased her with the tip of his tongue. Only tasted her sweet passion…

Then he pulled back, grabbed a condom from the

bedside table and sheathed his cock. She reached up for him, pulling him down for a kiss that was all tongue. He groaned. But then she pushed him back, her palms flat against his chest.

Was she only teasing him? Wasn't she going to let him find his release?

He might lose his mind if she didn't. But she only repositioned on his bed, rising up on her knees and turning her ass—that sweet ass that he found so damn irresistible—toward him.

"Damn, woman…" he murmured.

She was so seductive, so beautiful. She'd literally brought him to his knees. He rose on them and leaned over her. Then he slid inside her—into the heat and wetness that enveloped him.

He thrust hard and deep—going so far inside that he couldn't tell where he ended and she began. They moved as one. He thrust and she pushed her hips back, matching his every move. Then he reached beneath her, first caressing her breasts before sliding his hand lower to tease her clit.

She screamed as she came. And after a couple more deep strokes, the tension finally broke and he came—echoing her cry of pleasure. He collapsed onto his side, pulling her down next to him, their bodies still connected. His arms tightened around her.

"I'm not letting you go," he said.

She tensed. And so did he as he heard the words he'd spoken. He wasn't talking about forever. Eventually he would let her go. He would have to—because she was too dangerous, too manipulative. He couldn't risk falling for a woman like her. He couldn't…

10

"YOU LOOK HAPPY," her mother remarked. "Have you met someone?"

Of course Mandy Hamilton would think the only thing that could make Fiona happy was a man. But that wasn't the case. Her euphoric mood had nothing to do with Wyatt.

Not really…

But she raised her menu so her mother wouldn't see her face and the telltale blush she felt heating her skin. Fortunately, she'd met her at a pretty nice restaurant, so the menus were big. There were tablecloths, too, draped almost to the hardwood floor. Fiona wished she could crawl under that, as well, but then her mother would know something was going on with her.

"Why would you automatically think it has to be a man making me happy?" Fiona asked. "Why couldn't it be my job? Or my friends?"

Her mother uttered a tired sigh.

And Fiona lowered the menu to see weariness etched in her mother's face. Her usually smooth skin was pulled tight around her mouth and her brow was furrowed.

Reaching for her wineglass with a trembling hand, Mandy said, "I'm not trying to offend you."

But it usually happened when they got together, as they had today for lunch. Fiona had tried to get out of it by saying she'd had an appointment. But that damn Rita had already told Mandy Fiona's afternoon was open before she'd transferred her.

Matthew obviously harbored resentment over Fiona leaving him when they were kids. Maybe Fiona harbored resentment of her own—that her mother hadn't fought harder to keep her. Of course, her grandparents had had more money for that fight—for their lawyer and maybe even for the judge. They had thought what they were doing was right. They still thought that. And because Fiona loved them, she had put her resentment of them aside. She didn't visit them as often as they liked, though. Since she'd put aside her resentment of them, she needed to do the same with her mother.

"I know, Mom," she said. And she reached across the table to squeeze her mother's hand. It was small and callused. After her second husband had died, she'd had to take on another job—cleaning hotel rooms when she wasn't working the front desk. As an explanation and to make her mother happy, too, she shared, "I think I may be getting through to Matthew."

Her mother's brow furrowed more. "About?"

"I may be able to get him to go back to college and forget about this whole firefighter thing." Surely Wyatt would help her convince her brother. The way he made love to her, the way he held her afterward…

And not just that day she'd gone to his house wearing nothing but a coat and lace. They'd slept together every day since for the past week. Of course, they actually did very little sleeping. He came to her house, too. Unfortunately, he wore more than a coat. But it didn't matter; she undressed him quickly.

She was getting to him. He craved her as much as she craved him—his kiss, his touch, the way he filled her, the mind-blowing pleasure he gave her...

That was probably what her mother had noticed. That she was satiated. Mandy's mistake hadn't been feeling attracted to men who sought danger. Her mistake had been in falling for them. Fiona was wiser than her mother. Or maybe thanks to her mother, she was wiser. She wouldn't make the mistake of falling for Wyatt Andrews.

She was only using him.

Mandy smiled. "Matt wants to become a firefighter like that friend of his? His *big brother*—Wyatt."

"Wyatt isn't his big brother," Fiona snapped. Because that would make everything creepy and weird. "He's his mentor." And soon he would be mentoring him to return to college.

"There's a good-looking man," Mandy remarked with a lustful sigh.

That was creepy and weird, too—that she was attracted to the same man her mother was. She reached an unsteady hand for her water glass and regretted that she never ordered wine with lunch.

"I didn't realize your brother wanted to become a firefighter," Mandy continued.

Fiona had been preoccupied with worry that she had a bad relationship with her brother. She hadn't realized that the relationship between mother and son was strained, too. "Don't you talk to him?"

Mandy shook her head. "He only comes around to get his mail occasionally."

"Then where's he been staying?" Fiona asked.

"At school."

"Mom, he left school."

Mandy shrugged. "He may have left school, but he must still have the lease for his apartment. Or maybe he's been crashing with friends."

"You don't even know where he's living?" This was why her grandparents shouldn't have taken her away. She had always been more of a mother to her younger sibling than their actual mother had been.

"He's an adult, Fiona," Mandy said defensively. But in whose defense? Matthew's or her own? She was just as sensitive to Fiona's remarks as Fiona was to hers. She had probably taken her comment as a criticism, and rightfully so. "He can make his own decisions. I was his age when I married your father."

Fiona snorted. "You just made my point for me. He's too young to be making such serious decisions. And so were you."

"I was in love," Mandy said. And there was no defense now. Only sadness and loss haunting her blue eyes. "When I first saw you walk into the restaurant today, I thought maybe you would finally understand that."

"Why?"

"Because I thought that was why you looked so happy…" She held up a hand to ward off an interruption Fiona hadn't even been about to make. "I know your job makes you happy. And your friends make you happy. But that kind of happiness is different."

"What kind?" Sexual satisfaction? Because then she was deliriously happy.

"Love," Mandy said with a wistful sigh. "Nothing makes you happier than being in love."

Fiona's pulse quickened to a frantic pace, and she was the defensive one now. "I'm not!" She forced herself to draw a breath and relax. "I'm not in love."

"That's too bad," Mandy said. "You really don't know what you're missing."

"How can you say that?" Fiona asked. "You buried two husbands. Doesn't that prove to you that falling in love is too risky?"

Mandy waved her hand again—this time in dismissal. "Everything we do in life has some sort of risk to it. We shouldn't be afraid to live—or to love—because we might get hurt."

Fiona couldn't see it as her mother did. She saw only the bereaved young widow who'd cried hysterically beside two graves. And she saw now the woman who, albeit still beautiful, looked older than her years. She was tired and broken; that was what love had done to her.

No, that wasn't a risk Fiona was willing to take.

"You look miserable," Wyatt said as he stepped inside his boss's office to find the man bowed over his desk. The fire Braden had predicted weeks ago had yet to happen...

Unless Braden had sensed a certain redhead coming into Wyatt's life to burn up his sheets. Then it had happened. And Wyatt couldn't wait for it to happen again.

Braden glanced up from his desk. His eyes were so

bloodshot that Wyatt might have thought he'd been crying if not for the bottle of bourbon sitting at his elbow.
Drinking on the job? Some previous Hotshots members
had tried it—to deal with the danger and the difficulty
of the job and with their marriages falling apart back
home. But he had never seen the Huron Hotshots team
superintendent in such a condition before—not even
when he had first shared that he was getting a divorce.

Not wanting anyone else to see the boss in this condition, Wyatt shut the door behind himself. "What the
hell's wrong with you?"

Braden tossed an envelope across his desk. Wyatt
caught it and pulled the invitation from it. He read the
card in disbelief.

"What the hell?"

"She's getting married again."

"I know," Wyatt said. "I read the card. But why the
hell did you get an invitation?"

Ami's flowery penmanship had spelled out *Braden
Zimmer* on the envelope. He hadn't received it in error.

"They kindly request the honor of my presence."
Braden bitterly repeated what the card so callously
asked. His hand shook as he reached for his glass.

But Wyatt caught his wrist. "This isn't the answer,
you know."

"Your suggestion isn't the answer, either," Braden
said. "Going out to find another woman…" He flicked
the card Wyatt had dropped back onto his desk. It shot
across the room. "Like she found another man. She had
to have been seeing him while we were still together."

Wyatt sighed. "You know it happens. Hotshots are
on the road a lot." The danger—and the absences—

were why so many of them were given the ultimatum.
Give up the job or the marriage.

"She never complained," Braden said. "She never
minded when I was gone." He snorted. "Now I know
why…"

"I'm sorry, man."

"Why?" Braden asked. "You're right. You've been
right all along. Marriage and this job don't mix." He
pushed a shaking hand through his hair. "Crazy part
is that I thought we were good—until she told me she
was leaving. She said it was nothing that I'd done. It
was all her…"

"She was right," Wyatt said. "You didn't do anything wrong."

"I thought she would come back," Braden admitted. "Even after I gave her the ultimatum, that if she
left I wouldn't take her back, I thought she would call
my bluff. I thought she would come back."

Now Wyatt understood the devastation. Until that
invitation had arrived, Braden had been harboring hope
for a reconciliation and love for his ex-wife. Now both
were gone.

He picked the invitation up from the floor. "When
is this thing?" he asked.

"I guess she debated whether or not to send out the
invitation," Braden said.

She should have never sent it out at all. It was beyond insensitive; it was cruel.

Braden continued, "Because I just got it and the
wedding is next week."

"I'll be your date," Wyatt offered. And he'd plus one
his fist into the groom's cheating mouth.

As if he'd read Wyatt's mind, Braden laughed. "I don't want to ruin her day."

"Why not?" He couldn't still love her? Not after this?

Braden sighed. "It's not her fault that she wasn't in love with me." He pushed aside the glass and the bottle and repeated what he'd said earlier, "You're right."

"Yeah, we should go tear up that reception. You take out the groom and I'll kick the ass of the best man."

Braden laughed. "You're crazy."

"You just said I was right," Wyatt reminded him. How much had the man had to drink?

"You're right about women," Braden said. "There's no point in getting serious."

A chill of unease raced through Wyatt. He'd been with Fiona every night since she had showed up on his porch in just her coat and a couple of bits of lace. But they weren't serious...

"They break your heart and your spirit," Braden continued, his voice gruff with bitterness. "Even when you think it's real, it's not..."

Wyatt knew what he and Fiona had wasn't real. It was just a game. Her playing him to get her way, and his playing along to get her.

"Come on," he said, "let's get you out of here. Get you some coffee and food." It wasn't as if he had plans with Fiona. It was just that they usually wound up together. But not tonight.

Tonight his friend needed him. He ignored the protest of his body that reminded him he needed Fiona, too. He needed to be inside her, part of her...

Braden shook his head. "I'm fine."

"You're a mess," he replied with brutal honesty. "You need to sober up."

Braden pointed to the wedding invitation. "That sobered me up. I'll never get drunk again."

Wyatt picked up the half-empty bottle. "So why is most of this gone?"

"I wasn't talking about alcohol," Braden said with a little chuckle and a hiccup. "I'll never get drunk on love again."

Wyatt shook his head. "Come on, you need some coffee and food."

Braden planted his hands on his desk to push himself out of his chair. He caught himself as he swayed.

Wyatt came around the desk to help hold him up so that he wouldn't fall.

"You need a cold shower," Wyatt said. Maybe he'd take one himself—so that he would stop aching for Fiona. So that he wouldn't fall, either—for her.

"I don't expect you to know what I'm talking about," Braden said as he unsteadily walked around his desk. Wyatt had hooked his arm beneath the captain's to help guide him. "You've never been in love. You've never had that *need* to be with someone as much as you can."

"That's not love," Wyatt said. "That's lust."

Braden uttered a sigh of pity. For Wyatt. "You keep telling yourself that…"

The captain was drunk. He was making no sense. But Wyatt was cold before he ever stepped under the spray of icy water. He'd faced down some monster fires in his life. But he'd never been as scared as he was now.

What if it was already too late for him? What if he was beginning to fall for Fiona?

11

Fiona rolled over in bed—alone—and reached for her phone again. She had checked it just a few minutes ago, so she wasn't surprised to find that there were no new messages. Her hand shaking slightly, she scrolled through her old texts.

I'm sorry. Her mother.

She had already texted back: Me, too.

She would have to find a better way to deal with her mother. Mandy meant well; it wasn't her fault that they were so different. Fiona had thought that concern for Matthew might be the middle ground they needed to find, but it was clear they didn't share that concern. Her mother didn't even know where her son was living.

Because he hadn't answered her call, Fiona had sent a text to her brother: We need to talk.

He hadn't texted back—of course.

There was another text from Howard: I'm sorry you weren't aware that we weren't exclusive. We need to talk.

She hadn't answered, just as she hadn't answered any of his previous texts.

Haven't heard from you. Hope you're busy getting busy with the firefighter. Tammy.

Fiona would have texted her back, but she hadn't heard from the firefighter tonight. And while she checked again, she found no texts from him.

Was there a fire? Had his local fire crew or the Hotshots been called out?

He'd mentioned that the captain had some sixth sense that told him a big fire was coming. She'd thought he was joking, as he usually was. But there had been none of the usual amusement twinkling in his blue eyes.

"He's never been wrong," Wyatt had claimed.

Her pulse quickened with fear. So what if that was where he was now? Fighting some dangerous fire.

Maybe she should have texted him. But she hadn't wanted to bother him. Or distract him...

But she was distracted. Too distracted to sleep.

Maybe she should give up trying and drive by his place. He could be there. She hadn't checked earlier because lunch with her mother had unsettled her. She wasn't in love with Wyatt.

She knew better than to fall for a man like him. She would worry about him too much—like she was worrying now. Maybe needlessly—if he was home, probably sleeping soundly without a thought of her.

That was fine.

She was fine.

Then the doorbell rang. Startled, she gasped and jumped. She tossed back her blankets, pulled on her robe and headed for the front door. Her bare feet slipped on the highly polished hardwood as she hurried across her living room. The floor was natural with only a thick layer of polyurethane to protect it. So the color was just a shade darker than the walls, and the couch and wing-back chairs.

The motion light on the porch had come on, but she could only see a dark shadow through the sidelight beside the steel door.

Maybe it was Matthew. To a twenty-year-old, midnight was early.

Or maybe it was…

The shadow moved, stepping away from the front door. Before he could leave, Fiona unlocked and jerked open the door. "Hello?"

The dark shadow stopped at the top of the stairs leading down to her driveway. The porch light illuminated the back of his jacket, making the yellow glow like neon. Across the yellow, red letters spelled out *Hotshots*.

"Wyatt?" She hoped it was him. It looked like him. But there were nineteen other guys on the team. It could have been one of them, bringing her bad news. Though she doubted that she was on Wyatt's emergency call list. She wasn't anything to him.

The broad shoulders tensed. But he turned around, his handsome face more serious than she'd ever seen it.

"It's late," Wyatt said. "I shouldn't have come…"

"You're here," she said. He wasn't off fighting a fire; he wasn't in danger. But she was still worried that she was losing him, which was weird because she'd never really had him. She held out her hand to him. "Don't go…"

In two long strides he closed the distance between them and wrapped his huge hand around her small one. His skin was cold, so cold that it surprised her.

"Have you been outside very long?" she asked. Had he been standing on her porch before he'd rung the bell?

"I took a cold shower earlier," he said.

She smiled. "You didn't need to do that," she told him as she led him inside the warmth of her house and shut the door behind them. "You could have just come over here sooner."

"I didn't want to come over here." He dropped her hand and shoved both of his into the pockets of his coat—as if to stop himself from reaching for her again.

She blinked against a sudden stinging in her eyes. It wasn't tears. She wouldn't cry over Wyatt Andrews.

"I didn't ask you to come," she said. And she was grateful now that she'd hadn't texted him. He wouldn't have appreciated her sounding desperate and needy—which was unfortunately how he'd made her feel.

"After taking care of Braden, I intended to go right home," he said. "But I couldn't bring myself to drive past here without stopping…"

"Taking care of Braden?" she asked. "Is he okay?"

"No," Wyatt said, his voice gruff with concern and anger.

She ached for him again—for his worry over his friend. "What happened? Did he get hurt?" Maybe there had been a fire tonight.

"He's devastated," Wyatt said. "The ex-wife he still loves sent him an invitation to her wedding."

Fiona understood his anger now, and feeling some of her own, she replied, "Bitch."

"Yeah…"

She also understood why he hadn't intended to come

over tonight. "You should have stayed with him," she said. "Made sure he's okay."

"He was better once I sobered him up with a cold shower at the firehouse."

She already knew that the team took care of each other. "You think he'll be okay alone?"

"He'll be better alone than with a woman like her," he said.

That wasn't what she'd meant, but before she could clarify, he added, "Or a woman like you…"

Now she tensed, and the anger she felt was for herself, not on behalf of anyone else. "A woman like me? I am not a bitch like Braden's ex-wife."

He shook his head. "No, no, you're not," he quickly agreed. "It would be easier if you were…"

Was he breaking up with her? But then they would actually have to be together to break up. And they weren't together.

"Easier?" she asked. "If you want to end this…"

"What is *this*?" he asked.

She shrugged. "I don't know."

"I won't fall in love with a woman like you," he said, as if he were warning her.

Breath caught in her lungs with a gasp, but she released it in a shuddery sigh. "That's good," she said. "I don't want you to fall in love with me—because I would never fall in love with a man like you."

He released an unsteady breath of his own. "Because your statistics have all proven that I'm too great a risk?"

Apparently he was well aware of what he was to her: too great a risk. But she had to ask, "What is a woman like me?"

"A woman who would suck me in like so many of my friends have been," he said. "She acts like she's okay with his job—that she understands his calling. But then when he's totally in love with her, she starts issuing ultimatums—starts manipulating him to quit the team."

"Because she loves him and doesn't want to lose him," Fiona said—in defense of *women like her*.

"If she loved him, she would understand that the job—the team—is what makes him who he is," Wyatt said. "If she loved him, really loved him, she would respect that. She would respect that his career is more than a job to him."

Playing devil's advocate for women like her—women Wyatt apparently considered the devil—she said, "But if she doesn't love him, why would she try to get him to give up his dangerous career? Wouldn't she just let him keep it?"

"She wants to control and change him," Wyatt said with a bitterness she'd never heard from him before tonight.

"Has a woman ever tried that with you?" she asked as she wondered about the depth of his bitterness.

He shook his head. "I've never put myself in that position. I've never dated a woman like you before—for that very reason."

"We're not actually dating," she pointed out. "We haven't gone out to dinner or a movie. We've only gone to the bedroom."

His head jerked up and down in a quick nod. "That's right. *This*…isn't dating."

"It's just sex." But even as she said it, she recognized it as a lie. Before she could figure out what this was, though, he was shrugging out of his jacket and reaching for her.

"It's just sex," he agreed. But the tension had not eased from his handsome face. His jaw was still tense beneath the stubble.

So she repeated the lie. "It's just sex…"

He leaned down and pressed his mouth to hers— kissing her hungrily. He parted her lips and thrust his tongue inside.

Desire overwhelmed her. She lifted her arms and locked them around his neck—which was good because he lifted her. She held on as he carried her to the bedroom.

He glanced down at the slightly rumpled bed. "Were you sleeping?" he asked. "Did I wake you?"

"I wasn't sleeping," she assured him and admitted, "I was thinking about you." Worrying about him. But she kept that to herself. Instead, she pulled off his T-shirt and reached for the button of his jeans.

His hand replaced hers. He undid the button and zipper and kicked off his jeans. Then his boxers followed, and he stood before her gloriously naked. He was so fit—so perfect. But his job demanded that he be; he had to carry heavy equipment. And sometimes he had to carry people—if his team had been sent in to rescue.

That was why he carried her so easily.

"I was thinking about this…" She pressed her lips to his heavily muscled chest. And she felt his heart beating, pounding hard beneath her mouth. She licked his flat nipple. She continued down his body, caressing and kissing his rock-hard abs, his thighs. Then she focused on his erection. He was so aroused that his cock pulsed and jumped as she circled him with her fingers.

He groaned.

Then she slid her lips around him.

And he groaned again. His hands unsteady, he gripped her shoulders. "Fiona…"

She took him deep in her mouth, stroking him with her lips—teasing him with her tongue. She had wanted to ease the tension that she'd noticed in him the moment she'd found him walking away from her front door.

But he tensed more. Then his hands gripped her shoulders and pulled her up—to her feet. "I want you," he said. "I need to be inside you."

He reached for his jeans and pulled out a condom. She took it from his hand, tore the packet open with her mouth and slid it over his cock. While she did, he untied the belt of her robe and pushed it from her shoulders. Discovering that she wore nothing beneath it, he breathed, "Damn, woman…"

His hands moved, sliding gently over her body. He traced her curves, running his palms along her hips and thighs before he cupped her butt. Then he lifted her. As she wrapped her legs around him, he thrust inside her—joining their bodies.

He was so strong that he easily supported her weight as she slid up and down, teasing him and herself, building the tension in both of them. Her breasts pushed against his chest, where the light hair covering his muscles rubbed her nipples.

She moaned at all the sensations rippling through her, overwhelming her. And that tension she'd seen in him built in her now. She squirmed against him, trying to take him deeper. She gripped his shoulders and wound her legs tighter around his lean waist. Because she clung to him, he didn't need to hold her any longer.

And his hands moved over her. All over her...

One hand stroked down her back, his fingers tracing her spine to her butt. Then he moved them between her legs—even as he continued to press inside her. His hands were so big, his fingers so long, that he was able to stroke her clit.

And his other hand moved down the front of her body and over her breast. He cupped it in his palm, making her heart beat even faster. His hands were so strong, so rough from the hard work he did, that even his palm stimulated her nipple. He moved it back and forth, teasing her to madness. The tension was so unbearable that tears of frustration burned her eyes.

Then the fingers stroking her clit lightly pinched it. She tensed, then shuddered as she came—the orgasm slamming through her. "Wyatt!" His name left her lips on a scream of pleasure.

He uttered a guttural cry. And his body tensed before his cock pulsed inside her. His arms slid around her, holding her to him for a moment before he lifted her off and laid her on the bed. He disappeared into her bathroom a few minutes before returning. Even after sex, he still seemed as tense as he had earlier.

Over the past week, she'd learned that he took very little time to recover before he wanted her again—before he was hard and ready for her. So she reached for his hand and pulled him into bed with her.

She didn't wait, though. She began to make love to him with her mouth. As soon as her lips closed around his cock, it hardened.

His breath shuddered out and he murmured, "What are you doing to me?"

She didn't answer with words; she answered with

actions. She continued to slide her lips up and down the length of him. Then she took him as deep in her mouth, as deep in her throat, as she could. And she sucked him. At the same time, she stroked his thighs and hips and grasped his butt in her hands. But then he moved her, pulling her body around and over him so that he could reach her. He thrust his finger inside her and lapped at her clit with his tongue.

She shuddered as desire overwhelmed her. He sucked on her clit as he slid another finger in with the first. He stroked in and out of her. She tensed and then trembled as sensations raced through her again. As she came, she sucked him even deeper into her throat and slid her tongue around him.

He tensed and shouted as he joined her in release. Then he gently moved her around until she was in his arms, her head going naturally into the cradle of his neck and shoulder. And he held her.

This was so much more than sex. But she couldn't admit what it was—not even to herself.

INSTEAD OF EASING his tension, making love with Fiona had only added to it. It wasn't just sex—not anymore— if it had ever been. Somehow, despite that stress, he had managed to fall asleep. And it hadn't been for just minutes this time. When he woke he saw faint light creeping around her blinds; the sun would be rising soon. He had never stayed so long before. He slid out from beneath her and from between her satin sheets.

He'd been surprised the first time he'd come to her house and found red satin sheets on her bed. Everything about her was red-hot. Her body. Her beautiful face. Even her bed.

He hated to leave it. Hated to leave her. But he had already stayed too long. Hell, he probably shouldn't have come last night. Because no matter what they'd said, this was more than sex.

His heart hammering with fear over that realization, he dressed quickly. He needed to make a quick escape before he could change his mind, before he could give in to temptation and crawl back into bed with her and hold her until the sun rose fully.

He picked up his shoes so the soles wouldn't clunk against the hardwood floor. Carrying them, he hurried from the bedroom to cross the living room. Her house was very similar to his in the floor plan. But hers was tidier—nothing out of place. No clutter.

She was a neat freak. A control freak. Everything he'd known she was and feared. She wasn't the woman for him. And, as she'd already said, he wasn't the man for her.

Someday he might get an invitation in the mail as Braden had, asking him to her wedding to someone like the sleazy accountant. As Braden had, he'd probably get drunk and need one of the team to sober him up and talk him out of doing something stupid—like trying to stop the nuptials. Like trying to convince her that they could make it work.

It would never work. With a sigh, he reached for the knob and pulled open the door. But his escape was blocked. Matt stood in the doorway.

His eyes widened with horror as he took in Wyatt carrying his shoes. "What the hell—"

Despite how Fiona saw her little brother, the guy was an adult. So Wyatt wouldn't lie to him.

But Matt called him on his earlier lie. "You said

you'd never go for a woman like her! But now you're sleeping with her!"

"What your sister and I are doing isn't any of your business," Wyatt pointed out. At least he was sure that Fiona had never wanted her brother to know. Or she wouldn't have if she'd known how furious their liaison would make Matt. She wouldn't have risked her brother hating her.

Or maybe she would have, if she'd thought that ultimately she could protect him. There were so many dangers from which she would never be able to protect her brother. Car accidents. Illness. Heartbreak.

"It's all about my business," Matt insisted. "That's why she's sleeping with you. She wants you to make sure I don't get a spot on the Hotshot team."

Wyatt shook his head. "This has nothing to do with that." Because it wouldn't matter what anyone did; Matt couldn't make the team unless he was qualified. And he would never be qualified.

"Matthew," Fiona said as she rushed into the room. "What are you doing here so early?"

"You sent a text that you wanted to talk," Matt said. "Is this what you wanted to talk about? About how far you've gone to mess up my life again!"

"Matthew, I'm trying to make sure you don't mess up your life," she said. "Or risk it…"

"See," Matt said. "She admits what she's doing with you. Why do you keep lying?"

Wyatt saw the betrayal on the kid's face. He'd trusted Wyatt. He hadn't ever actually listened to him. But he'd trusted him, and by getting involved with Fiona, Wyatt had betrayed that trust. Before he could say anything, Matt turned and ran down the porch steps

and out to where he'd parked his beat-up old truck at
the curb.

"Go after him," she urged him. "Make sure he's
okay."

Wyatt turned toward her. He wanted to talk to her—
wanted to call her on her admission. Of course he'd
known she was using him. But…

"Please," she said. "Talk to him…"

She was right. Wyatt needed to talk to the kid.
Needed to calm him down. He nodded his agreement,
but as he turned away, he realized that whatever they'd
had was over.

She loved her brother too much to risk his hating
her. She wouldn't want to see Wyatt anymore, let alone
sleep with him.

He should have been relieved, but the tension was
back in his body, forming a tight knot in his guts. That
was just sex, though. That deep need and desire for her.

It wasn't love. He wouldn't be the fool Braden had
been and risk his heart on anyone. As soon as he saw
his boss again, and saw the misery on his face, Wyatt
would be happy he'd made his escape—that he was in
no danger of falling for Fiona.

12

THE DOOR TO her office opened with a creak. Fiona looked up quickly, but disappointment extinguished her faint hope. It wasn't Matthew standing in her doorway.

He hadn't talked to her in the week since he'd discovered Wyatt sneaking out of her house. Neither had Wyatt...

Maybe she was even more disappointed that it wasn't him who'd come to see her.

"Don't look so thrilled," Tammy said as she leaned against the doorjamb. She wore red today and looked exceptionally beautiful.

"I'm sorry," Fiona replied. "I'm just very busy."

"Bullshit." Tammy called her on it with the honesty borne of years of friendship. "You've been moping around for a week. It's Friday night. You're not working anymore." She came around her desk and opened the bottom drawer where Fiona kept her purse. She pulled it out by the strap and plopped it down in front of her. "You're leaving. Now."

"I have things I have to finish up—"

"Bullshit!" Tammy said again. She reached across

Fiona and pushed the power button on the monitor; the screen went black.

Like Fiona's mood.

"You need to get out of this office," Tammy insisted. "You need some fresh air and sunshine."

Her friend was right. Fiona needed to stop sulking in her office. She wasn't actually accomplishing anything but wallowing in self-pity.

She stood up and slung her purse over her shoulder. "Where are you taking me?"

"The club…"

"So much for fresh air and sunshine," she murmured. Not that the sun would be out much longer; it was already beginning to set outside her office window.

Tammy chuckled and slung her arm around Fiona's shoulders. "Okay, I should have said *alcohol and sexy men*."

Fiona tensed. There was only one sexy man she wanted to see. Was he mad at her? Did he believe what Matthew had—that she'd only been using him?

Guilt tugged at her. That was what she'd been telling herself. So was she a user or a liar?

"Stop thinking about the firefighter," Tammy admonished her.

She'd given Tammy a blow-by-blow of that horrible morning, and she'd kept her updated that neither man had contacted her again.

"I'm thinking about Matthew," she said—which was true, too. "I don't know if Wyatt caught up with him. I don't know what they talked about. And Mandy hasn't seen him, either," Fiona said. Which was no surprise, since their mother didn't even know where he was staying. If she did, Fiona could have tracked him down and

talked to him. Maybe she could have convinced him
that she had only his best interests at heart.

"That's why I need to talk to Wyatt," Fiona continued. "I need to see if he knows where Matthew is and
if he's okay." She had no doubt that Wyatt would know.
And she would have called and asked him for those
whereabouts, but she'd been afraid to call him. She was
worried that he was furious with her—as Matthew was.

She'd gotten used to her brother resenting her. She
didn't want Wyatt to hate her, too.

"You want to know more than that," her friend said,
calling her out on another lie.

She wanted to know if Wyatt was mad at her—if
that was why he hadn't called or texted or stopped by
to see her.

"Wyatt is Matt's mentor," Tammy continued. "Is he
even able to tell you what they talked about?"

"Matthew's twenty," Fiona reminded her. "I doubt
any of that applies any longer." She wasn't even sure
why or how Wyatt had become his mentor—or as her
mother called him, his big brother.

Tammy shrugged. "Their relationship is still built
on trust. Wyatt might not want to betray that."

The problem was that Matthew already thought he
had.

"I would be happy to just know if Matthew's all
right," she said.

"You'd know if he wasn't," Tammy insisted. "Someone would have called your mother."

Only if they needed to call his emergency contact.
And for all she knew, that could have been Wyatt, too.
But if Wyatt had been called for that reason, he would
have let her or Mandy know. She knew him better

now than she had before. She knew that, even though he acted cocky and funny, he cared about his friends. And he considered Matthew a friend.

She nodded. "You're right."

"What was that?" Tammy asked, cupping her ear and tilting her head as if she was hard of hearing.

So Fiona obliged with a shout and repeated, "You're right."

"I love the sound of that."

"But not about the place we should go," Fiona added.

"You don't want to go to the club?"

She shook her head.

"You don't want to see the fake firefighter again?" Tammy sighed. "Might be awkward for me to see the police officer, too."

Fiona thought the male strippers had only been an opening-night draw, but she didn't correct her friend's assumption that they'd be there. Instead she said, "I know another place we can go."

Tammy narrowed her brown eyes. "For fresh air and sunshine?"

"No," Fiona said. She gestured at the window and the darkening sky outside it. "Looks like the ship has already sailed on sunshine. I have something else in mind for us."

Tammy arched a brow.

"Alcohol and sexy men," Fiona said.

Tammy clutched her close again. "There's my girl bouncing back."

"And the best part about this place is that we'll probably be the only women."

Tammy whistled in appreciation. "I love it! I love

that we've been friends so long that you're starting to think like me."

The guilt she'd already been feeling—over how she'd used Wyatt—intensified. She had purposely misled Tammy into believing that she was ready to go out and meet men.

But then Tammy stopped and stared at her, her eyes narrowed with suspicion. "But if we're such good friends, how come you never told me about this place before?"

"I just found out about it myself," she admitted.

"What's it called?"

"The Filling Station." She tensed, afraid that Tammy might realize why she wanted to go there—if she was aware of its proximity to the local firehouse.

But her friend just smiled. "Sounds like I might get filled up tonight—with one of these sexy men you've promised will be there."

She wasn't sure who would be there. But she hoped Wyatt would be—and that he would give her a chance to explain. Now she would just have to come up with an explanation…

"It's my ex-wife's wedding day," Braden said. "But for some reason you look like the one who needs cheering up."

"I'm fine," Wyatt insisted. He tried to force his usual cocky grin, but his face hurt from the effort to smile. It was too difficult with the ache in his heart—in his body. He ached with missing Fiona. But he forced thoughts of her aside, as he'd tried to do all week, and focused on his friend. "Hey, we could go somewhere else if you'd rather…"

The Filling Station was louder than usual tonight with a euchre tournament taking place at the same time as a heated pool match in the back.

"Like the club where you got mistaken for a male stripper," he said.

Braden shook his head. "Hell, no. I'm not going back there."

"Technically I'm not sure we can," Wyatt admitted. "Since we took part in a brawl."

Braden snorted. "Brawl? That suggests we were actually able to fight back. Instead we got beat down…"

"And clawed up," Wyatt reminded him. He was glad that, for a moment, he was able to get his friend's mind off the wedding he shouldn't have been invited to attend. Now if only he could get his own mind off Fiona…

But she never left it. It was almost as if he could hear her. He glanced around and then he saw her, and he realized why the pool match in the back was so heated. Two men shoved at each other while a woman leaned over the table to take a shot.

He would recognize the sweet curve of that ass anywhere. It wriggled beneath the tight fabric of her little skirt.

"Speaking of brawls," Braden murmured.

The two men stopped shoving and started swinging. A brunette grabbed Fiona and tried to pull her away. But the men, locked in a wrestling move now, stumbled toward them and pushed the women back against the table. Trapping them there…

Wyatt cursed and jumped to his feet. Braden followed close behind him. He rushed up and grabbed one of the swinging men while Braden grabbed the other. The fists kept flying—this time nearly hitting him.

He ducked. And the man he'd grasped wriggled free and spun toward him. He dodged another blow.

"Hey, I got this," Braden said. And there was a particular gleam in his eyes. He needed this fight.

But Braden wasn't in the brawl alone. Cody and Dawson Hess, another Hotshot, rushed forward and stepped in, aiding their captain. So Wyatt turned his attention to Fiona, lifting her from the table and out of danger.

Dawson dropped his guy and reached for the brunette—pulling her away from the action, as well. He murmured something, but Wyatt didn't hear, or care, what he said. Fiona had all his attention.

"What is it with you, woman?" he asked.

Her arm had naturally looped around his neck, as it always had when he carried her off to bed—either his or hers. And she stared up at him through her thick, black lashes, feigning innocence. "What? I didn't start that fight."

"No," he agreed. She hadn't swung a punch, but she was the reason the men had started fighting—for her attention.

"Why can't men stay away from you?" he asked.

"I'm irresistible?" she said, as if she wasn't sure of the answer.

He was. She was definitely irresistible. Staying away from her for the past week had not been easy. He'd been tempted to act as crazy as Howard and blow up her phone with texts and voice mails. But he'd resisted.

He felt too damn guilty over her concern about her brother. If only he could be honest with her...

But he wasn't authorized to discuss any of the applicants. Not even with the applicants. Matt hadn't liked hearing that, either—back when he'd first told Wyatt that he'd applied to the forest service.

Someone bumped into his back, knocking him forward. He tightened his grasp on her. He didn't want to lose her again. "We're getting out of here," he said. And, amid catcalls and whistles, he carried her from the bar.

But even once they stepped out the door, he didn't release her. He kept carrying her. Maybe he would never let her go...

13

WYATT WAS THE irresistible one. He was the real reason that Fiona had gone to that bar—because she'd hoped to see him again. She had needed to see him again.

Seeing wasn't enough, though. She needed to touch and kiss him, too. But he hadn't carried her to his vehicle or hers. He hadn't carried her to one of their houses, either.

He had carried her to the fire station.

"Why did you bring me here?" she asked.

"Because it was closest," he replied as if his answer should have been obvious. But why did it matter what was closest? Especially if he was only rescuing her. Then he would have only needed to carry her away from the fight, not around the corner.

Maybe he wanted to talk to her—probably to give her a piece of his mind about how she'd manipulated him. Heat rushed to her face—from shame, not embarrassment. But he already knew why she'd done it. For Matthew...

She wanted to ask him about her brother—to make

sure that Matthew was all right. But if he wasn't, Wyatt would have contacted her. He would have told her.

And there was something she wanted to do more than talking about her brother or anything else. She tightened her arm around his neck and pulled his head down. She brushed her lips back and forth across his— teasing with butterfly-soft kisses.

He groaned and caught her bottom lip between his teeth. He nipped it lightly, then traced her lips with the tip of his tongue.

She moaned and clasped her hands behind his head, pressing his mouth to hers. She deepened the kiss, parting her lips wide, so he thrust all the way inside. Her tongue tangled with his. He drew back, or tried, but she sucked him deeper. Then she released him to nip at his lower lip.

He groaned. Then he dropped the arm from beneath her legs, so she slid down his body—her softness over his hard muscles. His hand at her back kept her clutched tightly against him, so tightly that her heels barely reached the floor. Holding her like that, flush against his body, he began to walk again. He moved through the garage of the fire station, past the bright yellow fire engines, to a room at the back.

He hit a switch with his fist and bathed the small, cement block room in light. "It's not pretty," he murmured. "But it was close."

It was an office. Similar to Captain Zimmer's. But the name on the desk placard was Wyatt's. Specifically: Assistant Superintendent Wyatt Andrews. He had an office at the firehouse, too.

Before she could ask him about it and his title, he

leaned down and kissed her again—as if he couldn't get enough of her lips. "I couldn't wait…"

Neither could she. She had questions she wanted to ask him. But he had already answered the most important one to her right now; he wanted her as much as she wanted him.

"I needed to taste your mouth," he said as he slid his tongue inside again. But he set her on her feet—finally—and stepped back.

She murmured a protest at the separation. But his hands were there, on the buttons of her blouse, undoing them. She'd left her coat at the bar, but Tammy would remember it.

Tammy! She'd left her friend in the middle of a fight. "I should go back," she murmured in faint protest, "and make sure my friend is all right."

"The brunette?"

"Yes."

"Dawson had her," Wyatt said. "He's used to extracting people who've gotten themselves into danger."

"Like you?" she asked.

"I'm getting better at it," he said, "thanks to the practice you've been giving me. For someone who likes playing it so safe, you've been finding a lot of trouble lately."

She couldn't deny it. She had been getting into trouble. And the biggest danger stood in front of her, parting her blouse. He pushed it off her shoulders and dropped it to the cement floor.

Usually she would have worried about the fabric wrinkling. But he was touching her, tracing his fingertips along the cups of her lace bra. And she couldn't care less about wrinkles anymore.

All she wanted was him.

He must have left his coat at the bar, too. He wore only a Forest Service Fire Department T-shirt and jeans. She dragged the T-shirt up and over his head and dropped it as carelessly to the floor as he had her blouse. Then she reached for his zipper. His erection pressed against the denim, demanding release. She obliged.

He sucked in an audible breath when her fingers slid over the tip of his cock—which had pushed out of his boxers. "Fiona…"

He lifted her again. And in the process he pushed up her skirt. It rolled up around her waist, leaving her ass bare but for the thin strap of her G-string. His hands slid over her butt.

"I love your ass," he murmured. And he easily snapped that lace string so that her underwear fell away, too. She clutched at his shoulders. They were so broad, so strong as he held her effortlessly—just as he'd carried her effortlessly for a block.

She wriggled and arched her hips. Tension wound so tightly inside her that her body begged for release. She opened her mouth to utter the plea for it—for him— when he kissed her again.

And as he thrust his tongue inside her mouth, he thrust his fingers inside her. She gasped at the pleasure. He swallowed that gasp and groaned as he deepened the kiss. His big, heavily muscled body shook slightly—as if he was as overwhelmed with desire as she was. Maybe his knees were as weak as hers were because he lowered her onto the bare surface of his desk. Wyatt Andrews was no paper pusher; whatever his duties as assistant superintendent entailed, it wasn't actually a desk job. It was a dangerous job.

But before she could dwell on that, he lowered his head to her breasts. Then he pushed down a bra cup with his mouth so that he could tease her nipple with his tongue—and his teeth. He scraped them across the sensitive point—back and forth—as his fingers stroked in and out of her. Then his thumb flicked across her clit, rubbing and teasing it, as he sucked her nipple into his mouth.

THE PRESSURE WOUND tightly inside her, and she clenched her muscles around his fingers. "Wyatt, please…" she murmured.

"Please you?" he asked. "That's exactly what I'm going to do." His thumb continued to rub her clit as his fingers thrust in and out. In and out. His tongue laved her nipple.

Pleasure crashed over her like a wave as she came. And she screamed his name again. He moved his lips from her breast, down her body. And he flicked his tongue inside her, as if tasting what he'd done to her. How crazy she was for him…

"Wyatt…" He was doing it again. Before she could catch her breath, he was rebuilding that need—that insatiable need—she had for him.

"Is the desk too hard?" he asked.

She shook her head. "No…"

"I am," he murmured, his voice gruff with desire. He fumbled a condom from his pocket, ripped it open and sheathed himself. Then he entered her in one swift move.

And the tension built again with each thrust. He

continued to tease her nipples and her clit. And within moments, she was coming again. "Wyatt!"

"You're so damn hot," he said. "So hot…"

She had missed him. So much…

She had especially missed how incredible he made her feel when they made love. But it wasn't love. It was just sex. Or that was what she wanted to believe.

His hands moved, sliding around to her butt again. He clutched it, driving her up and down his shaft in a flurry of thrusts. Then he shouted as his body tensed and he came.

"So damn hot…" he murmured between pants for breath.

He was the hot one—with sweat beading on his upper lip and making his shoulders and back slick. She brushed a fingertip across those beads, wiping them from his handsome face.

"That's what you do to me," he said. "You're the best workout I've ever had."

He was joking—as he always did. Even while Fiona told herself that, her pulse quickened.

"I should bring you upstairs to the showers with me," he suggested.

That was how she'd first imagined him naked—standing beneath a spray of water. She was tempted to agree—tempted to go with him wherever he wanted to carry her. But she didn't even know if they were alone.

Suddenly an alarm sounded—blaring out from within the station. She started as if she had been doused with icy water. She lost her breath for a moment as panic overwhelmed her. This was what he did—rushed out for fires.

Rushed *into* fires…

WYATT SAW THE fear on her face. "I'm sorry," he said. "We'll have to take a rain check on the shower…" He forced a hollow laugh at his lame joke.

She didn't even smile. She looked too shocked.

Was she worried about him leaving for a call? Or had she just been reminded that this was what her younger brother wanted to do—fight fires?

He had to wait for the other guys to arrive at the house. So he didn't have to move that quickly—yet. He pulled out and set her on her feet. She swayed, as if her legs were about to buckle. He caught her shoulders to steady her.

She tugged free. "You have to go," she said. But as she grabbed her blouse, shoved her arms into the sleeves and hurriedly buttoned it up, she looked like the one on her way to a fire.

"In a second," he said. He had already pulled his shirt on and zipped up his jeans. So he reached out to help her as she tried to roll her skirt back down her thighs.

Her face flushed bright red. She was either embarrassed that she couldn't manage it alone, or she didn't want him touching her. "I've got it…"

He wanted her. Again.

But he expected he might not get another opportunity. She had just remembered that he was the kind of man with whom she wanted nothing.

Nothing but help with her brother.

"I didn't find Matt," he told her.

She tensed. "You didn't?"

"No. He took off too fast that night," he said. Faster even than his sister was trying to take off now.

"You haven't heard from him?"

He shook his head. He didn't expect that he would, either. Matt had been furious with him—had felt betrayed. "I know where he's staying, though, so I'll wait until he cools off and go see him."

"Where?" she asked. "Where is he staying?"

Matt already felt as if Wyatt had betrayed him. If he told her where she could find the kid, Matt would never forgive him. "I can't…"

She cursed then. He had only heard her swear once before—when he'd told her about Braden's ex-wife sending him the wedding invitation.

"He's okay," Wyatt assured her. "We would have heard if he wasn't."

"You might have," she said. "Not me. My mother doesn't even know where he is."

His expression must have betrayed something because he saw the realization and the betrayal cross her face. "She knows."

He'd seen Matt's mom there before—cleaning up after her son as she'd done when he'd lived at home. "Since she didn't tell you, either, doesn't that convince you that Matt doesn't want you to know?"

"Why not?"

"Probably because he knows you'd call it a cockroach-infested frat house." Because that was what it was. Through the steel door, he could hear that the team was rushing in. He pulled open the door to his office.

And before he could say anything else, she pushed by him and hurried past the fire engines and the men pulling on their gear next to them.

Wyatt stepped out behind her. But he didn't chase her. He doubted he could catch her with the speed at which she was running away from him.

Cody whistled as she rushed past him. "Damn, Wyatt, how the hell do you always get so lucky?"

Braden snorted. "Lucky?" He obviously wasn't giving it the same connotation that Cody had. "I think he's a damn fool for ignoring his own advice."

Wyatt couldn't argue with his boss—partly because he was too busy jumping into his gear. Partly because he had been a hypocrite. No matter what he and Fiona claimed, what they had was more than sex.

But he suspected that was over now.

Cody gasped. "What? You think Wyatt is getting serious?" He jammed his hat on. Despite having all his heavy gear on, he shivered—with revulsion. "I thought that would never happen."

"It won't," Wyatt assured the others. At least it wouldn't now. "There's no danger of that."

The only danger was whatever fire they faced. And he preferred it that way. He was trained and equipped to handle his job. He couldn't handle Fiona O'Brien and all the feelings she inspired in him. They needed to be done.

14

THEY WERE DONE. Fiona was glad. Relieved, really…

He knew where Matthew was but refused to tell her. Sure, he believed he was honoring Matthew's wishes. But what about hers? Didn't he care about her at all?

He knew how worried she was about her brother— worried enough that she'd slept with him. And for what? He hadn't helped her.

"What's going on?" Tammy asked, snapping her fingers in front of Fiona's face. "You've barely touched your wine, so you can't be passing out on me."

Fiona blinked away the faint sting in her eyes and focused on her friend. They were at Tammy's place again. The brunette preferred it to Fiona's because she didn't worry if she dropped crumbs on the floor or spilled wine on the cushions.

Was Fiona that difficult? That uptight?

She flashed back to making love with Wyatt standing up. Lying on the desk. In the shower. She'd had wild, passionate sex with him in every position. She wasn't uptight with Wyatt. But she had been in other areas of her life.

"I'm sorry," she told her friend. *About so many things...*

Tammy waved a hand. "I forgive you for being distracted. Hell, after bringing me to that bar the other night, I would forgive you anything."

Tammy had wanted to go there tonight, but Fiona had refused to go back. "The Filling Station is a much better place than that club," she continued. "The men at the club were just dancers pretending to be heroes. You found the real heroes."

"Or fools..."

"They put their lives on the line to protect other people," Tammy said. "That's heroic."

"It's dangerous."

Tammy laughed. "Their call the other night was to put out a car fire. It's not as dangerous as you think."

"This time..." But there would be other calls—other fires. Statistics didn't lie. Firefighting was a dangerous profession.

Tammy shrugged. "I'm willing to risk it. You weren't the only one who got carried out of the bar the other night."

"Wyatt said Dawson had you."

"Dawson..." She said his name with a dreamy sigh. "All I got was a kiss before he had to rush off. But he called me later."

Wyatt hadn't called her. But then, he probably thought she was furious with him. And she should be. But he wasn't the only one keeping things from her.

"I left Mandy another voice mail," Fiona said.

"She hasn't called you back?"

"You know how my mother tries to avoid confrontation." That was probably why Mandy hadn't fought harder for custody of her; she didn't like to fight.

Fiona uttered a weary sigh. She didn't want to fight anymore, either. She took a sip of wine and asked her friend the question she'd silently asked herself moments ago, "Am I that difficult?"

Tammy tensed.

And Fiona had her answer before her friend said a word. So she apologized again. "I'm sorry…"

Tammy reached over and squeezed her knee. "Don't you dare! You're not difficult."

"Liar."

Tammy giggled. "You're not difficult with me," she said. "You accept me as I am." Tears shimmered in her brown eyes. "Not everyone approves of how I date…"

Her mother and sisters often gave Tammy a hard time and nagged her to find a husband, settle down and start a family.

"It's your life," Fiona said.

Tammy leaned back against the bright orange cushions behind her and nibbled on her bottom lip for a moment.

"What is it?" Fiona asked. "You know we can say anything to each other."

Tammy spoke slowly, for once, as if choosing her words carefully. "How can you accept me and the choices I make?" she asked. "And not accept your mom and brother and the choices they make?"

Fiona paused a moment to think. "I don't worry about you," she said.

Tammy laughed. "Why not? I'm not cautious like you are. I do *things* that I shouldn't."

"But you're strong," Fiona said. "I've never seen you

cry. I have never seen you down." She couldn't say the same of her mom and her brother. She had seen them both devastated. And she worried that she would again.

Tammy shrugged. "I just keep a positive attitude. I expect the best."

"But aren't you often disappointed?" Fiona wondered.

Tammy shrugged again. "I don't know. I don't dwell on the disappointments."

"How are we friends?" Fiona wondered.

"Bad habit?" Tammy asked as she held out her wineglass toward Fiona.

She clinked her glass against it. "The best."

Wyatt had been the best—the most amazing lover she'd ever had. Maybe that was why she couldn't stop thinking about him, why her body couldn't stop wanting his.

It was why she jumped when her phone dinged with a text. And wine sloshed over the rim of her glass. She cursed.

Tammy waved a hand in dismissal of the spill. "It's not a big deal."

Nothing was to Tammy. Maybe that was the attitude Fiona needed to adopt. Maybe she needed to care less about caution and more about people.

She glanced down at the text with surprise. Maybe this was the opportunity for her to try out Tammy's attitude.

"You have to go," Tammy said.

"Yes."

"No, I wasn't asking," Tammy said with a laugh. "I was telling you—you have to go. I have a hot date."

Fiona noticed, belatedly, the cute tight blue dress her

friend wore. "You look beautiful," she complimented her. "As always."

Tammy smiled. "Thanks."

"Dawson?"

Her smile grew wider. "Yes…"

Tammy wasn't a *woman like her*; Wyatt probably wouldn't oppose her relationship with his friend.

"You have a date, too," Tammy said, pointing at the phone. She wished. But she and Wyatt had never dated. They had never had a relationship. And they never would. But instead of feeling disappointed, she should be relieved.

She gave her friend a hug goodbye and needlessly wished her a good time. Tammy always had a good time.

Fiona wasn't sure she would ever have as good a time as she'd had with Wyatt. But she would survive. Nothing devastated her the way it did her family. Maybe that was why she and Tammy were such good friends; they were both strong. As she walked toward her car, she drew in a deep breath. She suspected she would need that strength now.

"You need to get back out there," Braden goaded him, deliberately tossing his words back at him. Just like that first day Fiona had showed up, they were in the weight room. But Braden was probably lifting more than Wyatt was. He was preoccupied. "It's not like you to brood over a woman."

No, it wasn't. But Fiona O'Brien wasn't just any woman. She was controlling and manipulative. And passionate and loyal. Her brother had no idea how lucky he was to have her love and devotion.

She would do anything for him.

Even Wyatt...

Despite her fear of his profession and lifestyle, she'd risked getting involved with him. For Matt...

Stupid kid.

Instead of appreciating how much she loved him, he resented her. He should be grateful that he had family who cared about him. Wyatt would give anything to bring his family back. But they were gone.

He shook off the uncharacteristic flash of self-pity. He had family: his Hotshot team. That was why he worried about them—especially Braden.

But his boss had just made it clear that he was doing better than Wyatt was.

A little defensively, he replied, "I'm not moping around." He wasn't mentoring, either. Maybe he'd been too subtle with Matt these past six years. Maybe it was time to throw away the psychology books and knock some sense into the kid.

He lowered the free weights to the floor. "I'm getting out of here."

Braden groaned. "Don't tell me that you're going to chase after the redhead."

"No," Wyatt assured him. "I'm actually going to the one place where I know she won't be."

Matt wouldn't have revealed his location or allowed his mom to, either. He wouldn't want his sister knowing where he was staying. But that was crazy; it didn't mean that she would have kept coming over.

Fiona knew where Wyatt lived and she hadn't been by. That was because she didn't love him, though. She'd only been using him—not for sex, but to influence her brother.

Wyatt had resisted getting involved before. But he shouldn't have. She hadn't been asking too much. The kid wasn't firefighter material. Not because of the danger, though.

Matt needed to stay in school and find a career that better suited him. And it was about damn time Wyatt told him. Sure, Matt would resist and probably resent him as much as he did his sister.

But Wyatt didn't care anymore.

He showered quickly and headed to the cockroach-ridden frat house in a town west of the national forest. But it was a wasted effort. According to one of the kid's several roommates, he'd gone to his mom's.

Wyatt knew where Mandy Hamilton lived. He'd picked Matt up there for four years—before the kid had gone to college. He pulled into the driveway on the right side of the ranch-style duplex. Matt's friend had told him the truth—because Matt's beat-up truck was parked half on the street, half on the grass. Wyatt had bought the clunker for Matt, and they'd worked on it together to get it running. Mandy's car was gone; she was probably working.

He shut off his truck and hurried up to the door—wanting to catch Matt before he left, too. He met the kid at the door—as he had when he'd been sneaking out of Fiona's house at dawn.

"Déjà vu," Matt remarked, his voice sharp with bitterness.

Wyatt shook his head. It wasn't the same—because he hadn't seen Fiona since that night at the firehouse. Maybe that was why he was so tense and edgy. Maybe it was because he was sick of the way the kid had been acting.

"Are you still going to try to tell me that you're not doing my sister?" Matt asked.

Not anymore. But that was none of the kid's business.

"I'm not an idiot," Matt said.

"Yes, you are," Wyatt said.

Matt's head snapped back as if Wyatt had struck him. He had always been encouraging to him—never harsh or critical. Maybe he'd acted more buddy than mentor. It was good that Wyatt had focused on firefighting rather than psychology.

"You're an idiot for not appreciating how much your sister loves you—"

"I don't need her kind of love," Matt said. "Just like I don't need your *mentoring* anymore, either." At twenty, it was his right to end their mentoring relationship. He was an adult now. The kid tried to edge around him.

But Wyatt blocked his way. "You do need my mentoring," he insisted. "You need me to make you appreciate having people in your life, family who love you."

"You think she loves me?" Matt asked. "She tries to manipulate and control me. If that's how she loves, then she must love you, too."

Wyatt sucked in a breath. But the kid was wrong. Fiona didn't love him.

"She was only using you, man," Matt said. "You—with your psychology degree—should have been able to figure that out."

He had. But he hadn't cared. Admitting to that would make *him* look like a user, though.

"What I've figured out," Wyatt said, "is that you resent her for something over which she had no control. She didn't want to leave when you were kids. Her grandparents and a judge forced her to leave."

"I know." But the petulance of his tone and the look on his face belied the claim.

"If she'd had the choice, she would have stayed," Wyatt said.

Matt shrugged. "Why? I would've gotten the hell out and never looked back, if it had been me. How do you know what she would have done? Did she tell you that? Did you two actually talk or just—"

Wyatt caught him—not with a blow—just with a hand clasping his shoulder tightly before Matt said something that would make Wyatt want to hit him.

"She didn't have to tell me," Wyatt said. "Her actions speak louder than words anyway. She came back. She wouldn't have done that if she'd actually wanted to leave. She wouldn't be trying to have a relationship with you if she didn't genuinely love you—especially with how obnoxious you've been to her."

Matt shook his head, and his lip curled with disgust. "I suppose that's why she slept with you, too—because she genuinely loves *me*."

It was. But Wyatt wouldn't share that with her brother. The kid already knew too much. Or at least he thought he did.

"Don't talk about her like that," Wyatt warned him.

"I don't want to talk about her at all," Matt said. "I don't want her in my life. And now I don't want you, either." He shrugged off Wyatt's hand on his shoulder. "I thought you were my friend." This time he didn't just try to edge around Wyatt, he shoved him out of his way and ran for his truck.

Where had the scrawny teenager he'd first met gone? When had the kid become a burly man?

Wyatt sighed.

"Thank you for trying," a soft voice murmured.

He glanced back at the house and found her standing in the doorway. Sunlight caught in her red hair, making it glow like fire.

Maybe that was why his heart stopped beating— for just a millisecond—as it did when he first saw the flames. When he wondered if he would survive the fire…

Usually he pushed aside that momentary fear— because he knew he would make it. He always did.

This time he wasn't as confident. This time he worried that the fire would get him—because he was falling for her.

15

"THANK YOU," SHE SAID, "for driving me home." She had invited him inside, which was probably a mistake. But it wouldn't be the first one she'd made. She'd made so many—probably just that day. "Mandy picked me up here earlier and brought me to her place so that Matthew wouldn't see my car when he came over to pick up his mail."

Wyatt nodded, but he seemed distracted—or nervous as he stood tensely in her living room. She'd forced herself to mess it up a little, so she would learn to live with it. There was a glass left out on the sofa table. She hadn't been able to bring herself to forgo the coaster, though. But the glass had been there before she'd left with Mandy.

She'd even messed up the pillows on the couch and hadn't folded the blanket. Her hands itched to straighten things now—probably because she was nervous. So she curled them into fists and held them against her sides. And she noticed that Wyatt had done the same. She doubted he wanted to straighten her living room. Maybe he'd done it so that he wouldn't reach for her.

They had never spent much time in her living room before—only as long as it had taken him to carry her across it to her bedroom.

Images rolled through her mind, and heat flashed through her. She had the sudden urge to fan herself—or to reach for Wyatt. But she forced her focus back to their conversation. Back to Matthew.

"My mother's little plan didn't work," she said. "The minute he saw me he forgot all about his mail. He was running out when you showed up."

"I'm sorry," he said.

"Why?" she asked. "You tried to talk to him."

Wyatt snorted derisively at his efforts. "Only because I physically stopped him from passing me on his way out."

"Thank you."

"For restraining your brother?" Humor glinted in his blue eyes.

And Fiona's pulse quickened. She loved his humor. She loved so much about Wyatt Andrews. "Thank you for defending me to my brother—for trying to explain why I…"

"Slept with me?"

She gasped. But she couldn't defend herself without admitting that sleeping with Wyatt had been more about wanting him than helping her brother. She still wanted him. And she was pretty sure that there was nothing either of them could do to help her brother.

He was too resentful and angry right now.

"I'm sorry," he said. "I was just kidding…"

He did that so much and until now, it hadn't occurred to her to wonder why. She had just thought it was his personality. But she'd heard something else in his voice when he had been talking to Matthew about family; she'd heard yearning.

"Were you kidding when you told my brother he should appreciate having family who loves him?" she asked, and as she asked, she studied his handsome face. If she hadn't been looking, she might have missed it—the brief flicker of a sorrow so intense it struck her heart.

And that yearning was in his voice again when he said, "That's what he should appreciate more than anything else in this world."

"Tell me about your family," she urged. They had shared and acted on every sexual desire with each other, but they had never actually talked—never had the kind of getting-to-know-you conversations people did when they were dating. But they hadn't been dating. They'd only been…

"You've only met a few of the guys," he said. "The ones that work out of this firehouse with me and Captain Zimmer—like Cody and Dawson. But our team is made up of twenty members."

Unaware that she'd even closed the distance between them, she reached up and pressed her fingers to his lips. "I'm not asking about your Hotshot team," she said. "I'm asking about your *family*."

The tension was back on his face, twitching in a muscle along his tightly clenched jaw. "The team is my family."

And she was beginning to suspect why even before he added, "They're the only family I've got."

"You were an orphan?"

He shook his head. "Not like Cody was an orphan," he said as if she knew it already.

She hadn't talked to Cody long enough for the man to tell her his life story. But she had spent time with Wyatt—a lot of time. She should have known about his life—about his past. But he'd never talked about it; he'd never shared with her. "You were an orphan," she said, amazed that he'd never mentioned it.

He shook his head. "After my parents died, I didn't have to live in foster homes. I had an aunt who raised me…great-aunt," he said, as if correcting himself. "She raised me until she passed away. But I was already in my first year of college then."

"Your parents died when you were a child," she said, her heart heavy with his loss and pain. Even the aunt who'd taken over for them was dead, too. "That made you an orphan. How old were you?"

"Almost twelve."

The same age she had been when a judge and her grandparents had taken her away from her family. Fortunately, her grandparents had been family, too. And they'd loved her—even if they hadn't respected her wishes.

She sucked in a breath. "That's so young."

"Weren't you younger than that when your dad died?" he asked.

She nodded. "But maybe that was easier, since I don't remember much about him." He'd always been gone—racing cars. Mandy had often left Fiona with her grandparents so she could travel with him. She'd been there the day her young husband's car had struck the wall and burst into flames. "And I still had my mom. I wasn't an orphan."

Not that Mandy had been around much after that— either physically or emotionally. She'd gone out a lot—trying to ease her pain. But when she'd fallen for Matthew's father and then lost the drummer to a drug overdose, she'd been in even more pain.

Wyatt finally unfisted his hands and reached out, closing them around her shoulders. She hadn't said anything—hadn't complained—but it was as if he knew. Maybe Matthew had told him. He clasped her close, giving her comfort when he was the one who needed it.

She clutched at his back, holding him as he held her. "How did your parents die?"

"Fire."

She gasped and pulled back. "What?"

"They'd gone out west for their second honeymoon— some little cabin in the middle of a national forest where they could be alone. They died together—in a wildfire."

He said it all so calmly, so matter-of-factly. But the pain was there, buried just beneath the surface. She heard it in the gruffness of his voice and saw it in the darkness of his usually bright eyes.

"I'm so sorry," she said, and she tightened her arms around him, trying to give him comfort. Trying to take away the pain she could still feel in him.

His broad shoulders moved as he shrugged off her sympathy. "It happened a long time ago."

"But it still affects you," she said. "Or you wouldn't do what you do. It's why you became a firefighter. Why you wanted to be a Hotshot. Right?"

"One of them—a Tahoe Hotshot—died trying to save my parents," he shared.

"Is that why you do it?" she asked. "You're giving your life for his?"

He shook his head. "I'm not giving my life up. It's not that dangerous."

She stepped back—out of his arms. "How can you say that? You just admitted that a Hotshot died. And he's not the only one. There was the whole team that—"

He pressed his fingers to her lips now. "You've given me this argument before."

As the reason why her brother shouldn't become a Hotshot. But it was also the reason why she hadn't wanted to fall for Wyatt. She worried now that it might be too late.

WYATT SHOULDN'T HAVE stopped her. He should have let her continue the argument that illustrated why they could never be together. She thought his job was too dangerous—so she would want him to quit. Even after he'd shared with her what he hadn't with anyone else, she still didn't understand him—didn't understand his need to do what he did.

To fight fires…

He also shouldn't have touched her. Because the feel of her silky lips beneath his fingertip was distracting him with thoughts—with memories—of how those lips felt beneath his. Or on his body…

He groaned. And then he replaced his finger with his mouth. Kissing her was another way to stop her argument. And to make himself feel better. In sharing his past with her, he'd opened up wounds he'd thought healed long ago.

Nearly twenty years had passed now. Why did he still miss them? Would he feel that way about her when they were over? Would he miss her for years?

She kissed him back with all the passion with which

she usually argued. Her hands moved through the hair at his nape, pulling his head down so that she could slide her mouth across his. She nipped at his bottom lip, then stroked her tongue over it but not quite into his mouth.

He groaned and lifted her, with one hand on her butt, the other holding the back of her head. And he deepened the kiss.

She wrapped her legs around his waist and rubbed her hips against the erection straining to break through his jeans. He had to have her. *Now.*

Instead of carrying her into the bedroom, he turned and lowered her onto the couch. As she lay back against the cushions, he pulled off his clothes.

She watched him—as if she was watching one of those damn dancers at the club. Her green eyes sparkled with amusement while she licked her lips. "I wish I had some dollars," she murmured.

"You don't need an excuse to touch me." He reached for her hand and wrapped it around his cock. Then questioned his sanity as he groaned. Nothing felt as amazing as her soft hand sliding up and down his shaft, gently stroking him. Then she wrapped her fingers tighter and pumped him.

He pulled back—afraid that he might come that quickly. And while his tense body begged for the release, he wanted to please her, too.

She wasn't wearing a skirt today but black, stretchy yoga pants that clung to every sweet curve of her hips and ass and legs. He almost regretted pulling them off...until he saw that she wore only a thin scrap of lace beneath them. She lifted her sweatshirt, pulling it up and over her head. The black lace bra matched her panties and highlighted the milky whiteness of her skin.

She was so damn beautiful. His breath caught in his lungs, making them and his heart ache. The sensation was worse even than when his oxygen was running low; this was as if there was no air at all. He fought the panic, the feeling that he was falling.

For her…

She must have tired of waiting for him to touch her…because she touched herself. First she pushed down the straps of her bra. As they dangled down her arms, she reached behind herself and unhooked it. The lace fell away from her body, leaving her breasts bare. But not for long. She cupped them in her palms. The mounds were so full that they spilled over her small hands. She played with her nipples, rolling them between her forefinger and her thumb. Back and forth, back and forth. They grew longer and redder as her passion built. Then she moved one hand away from her breasts, sliding it down her body until her fingers slipped beneath her panties. Through the lace, he watched her fingers stroke her clit.

She bit her bottom lip and arched as she pleased herself. His control snapped. And he tore away that lace and surged inside her. She was ready for him. She locked her legs around his back and rose up, meeting his every thrust. She rubbed her breasts against his chest and clutched at his back, her nails scraping deliciously over his skin.

He had never known as passionate a lover as his little redhead. She drove him out of his mind. So he kept driving into her body—deeper and harder—until she screamed. But it wasn't with pain—it was with ecstasy. Her orgasm flowed over his cock, hot and endless.

"Wyatt!" she gasped between pants for breath. "Wyatt..."

She said his name with awe—as if he was as special to her as she had become to him. Her hands gripped his butt, holding it tightly as he kept pumping into her body. And she came again, her green eyes wide with shock. "What do you do to me? Why is it always so amazing?"

He wished he knew. But he was afraid to delve too deeply because the answer might scare him. He couldn't think at all now. The pressure inside him had built to the breaking point. He was losing his mind. Then his body tensed, and his cock pulsed. He came so hard that it racked his body; he shuddered and shouted.

Her name...

And he realized that he wasn't in danger of just losing his mind. He was in danger of losing his heart, too.

He'd braced his arms against the couch to hold his weight off her; now they shook with reaction. He eased out of her and off her and stood up.

"Where are you going?" she asked, as she reached for him. "The bedroom?"

He wanted to. So badly.

He wanted to carry her to her bed and make love to her all over again. But that feeling in his chest hadn't eased. If anything, it was harder to breathe. Panic gripped him.

He was falling for her. He couldn't deny it anymore. He couldn't ignore it. He could only run from it.

He cleared the passion and the fear from his throat and replied, "The firehouse."

Disappointment dimmed the brightness of her green eyes. "Really?"

His hands still shaking, he reached for his clothes and turned away from her to put them on. He couldn't look at her—lying there naked, her creamy skin flushed from their lovemaking. He couldn't look at her and not want to be with her again.

Still. Forever...

But he, better than most, knew there was no such thing as forever.

"I have to go," he reiterated. "Braden's been having that strange feeling..."

"You told me about that," she said. "That he thinks a fire's coming. But he's had that feeling for weeks, and nothing has happened but that little car fire."

Wyatt nodded. But then he pressed a fist against his heart. "But I have it now..."

"You think a fire's coming, too?"

The fire had already come—stomping into the firehouse in her red heels. And he'd already been burned. Now he just had to make sure that it didn't consume him completely.

16

FIONA HAD SEEN Wyatt restless—like the night that his friend had received the wedding invitation to his exwife's nuptials. She had seen him vulnerable—when he'd told her about the tragic deaths of his parents. But she had never seen him the way he'd been as he'd hurried out of her house: scared.

What had scared him?

Was there actually some monster fire starting out there that he and his captain were mythically able to sense?

Or was he scared that he'd been vulnerable with her? That he might be falling for her, too?

She had fallen for him—so deeply. She had been falling even before he'd shared that most vulnerable part of himself with her—his pain.

His motivation. She understood now why he did what he did. It wasn't for the reasons her brother had wanted to become a Hotshot—for the thrill of danger, or the glory, or the women. It was because of what had happened to his parents and to the Hotshot who'd tried to save them. Maybe he'd figured that if he'd been there, he could have saved them. Or maybe it was like what she'd accused him of. He wanted to devote his life to the one lost trying to save his family.

Guilt tugged at her now—for all the things she'd thought him: cocky, arrogant, superficial, careless.

He was none of those things. He was a good and honorable man. And she'd misjudged him so badly.

She owed him an apology for her misjudgment and for using him. She had destroyed his relationship with her brother. She had screwed up everything she'd set out to do.

She owed both Wyatt and Matthew an apology. While she didn't agree with her brother's reasons for wanting to emulate Wyatt, she understood why he would want to be like the firefighter. Wyatt Andrews was an amazing man.

Wanting to apologize to them both, she hurriedly showered and dressed again—in jeans and a soft green sweater. She was reaching for her purse when she heard heavy footsteps cross her porch.

Her heart lifted. He had come back to her.

But when she pulled open the door, it was her brother who stood before her. And he seemed even angrier than he had been during their brief confrontation earlier. His body bristled with it. When he lifted his arm, she instinctively stepped back, almost afraid that he might strike her.

Instead he waved a paper in her face. "You got what you wanted, *sis*," he said. "I hope you're happy now."

"What are you talking about?"

"After you and Wyatt left," he said. "I went back to Mom's to get my mail." And probably to give Mandy a piece of his mind for setting up the ambush.

Fiona had hardly been able to believe it when her mother had texted an offer to set up a meeting between her and Matthew. Mandy had agreed that they needed to talk. She'd also wanted to mend fences with Fiona over not admitting that she'd known where he was staying. While she'd mended fences with one child, she'd destroyed them with the other.

She owed her mother a thank-you and an apology.

Matthew clutched the paper so tightly in his hand that it crumpled and tore. And his face flushed with anger. "This was waiting for me."

"This?"

"My rejection letter from the Forest Service Fire Division."

She grabbed the letter from his hand. And the first thing she noticed was the date in the corner. It had been printed two days before she had even confronted Wyatt at the fire station. "When did you get this?"

"Just now," he said. "I haven't been by Mom's in a while, so I don't know how long it was sitting there."

"Do you have the envelope?"

His brow furrowed with confusion. But he pulled a wad of paper from the pocket of his jeans.

She grabbed the torn envelope from his hand and pointed out the postmark date. It must have been sitting among their mother's junk mail for weeks. It had been printed and mailed before Fiona had ever talked to Wyatt. "I thought this hiring process was supposed to take months?"

That was what he'd told her when he'd first admitted to applying. That was one of the arguments she'd used for him to stay in school—in case he had been rejected. But he had been so certain that, with Wyatt's

control over you, either," she sadly realized. "You're going to keep hating me over all those things that were beyond my control. I can't change the way you feel about me."

But seeing that letter had changed the way she felt about Wyatt. She had begun to think that he was a good man. An honorable man. But he'd used her. Sure, she'd been using him, too. But…

Her temper ignited, and she grabbed the envelope and letter back from Matt. Then she picked up her purse and keys and headed toward the door.

"Where are you going?" he asked.

"To give Wyatt Andrews a piece of my mind…" And maybe another slap in the face.

DESPITE HAVING JUST had sex—amazing, hot and crazy sex—with Fiona, Wyatt was still tense. So stressed that he was pounding the bag in the firehouse gym.

"There's nothing on the radar," Braden said.

"Does that make you feel better?" Wyatt asked.

Braden shook his head. "No."

"It's out there." Wyatt wasn't sure if he actually believed it or just hoped that there was. Sure, he hated fires—probably more than most. But he would welcome the distraction of fighting one. Not a monster like Braden kept claiming was on its way. Maybe another car fire on the edge of some remote road…

Something that would sound an alarm and snap Wyatt out of his preoccupation with thoughts of Fiona. With feelings for Fiona—feelings he didn't want.

"Are you sure it's a fire that's bugging you?" Braden asked. Of course he would be suspicious.

Wyatt had never claimed to have any fire-sensing ability before. He wasn't like Braden.

And Braden knew that. But since his boss had already called him a hypocrite, Wyatt refrained from sharing anything with him.

Braden chuckled. "She got to you."

Wyatt punched the bag harder—so hard it nearly snapped back and caught him in the face. The bruise from the woman's shoe had faded long ago. And Fiona's slap had never left a bruise. But maybe he needed a blow upside the head now. He needed something to knock some sense into him. He could never have a future with Fiona. She would never be able to accept his career.

A strong hand squeezed his shoulder. "You poor bastard…"

Wyatt shrugged off his hand. "Screw you."

Braden chuckled again. "You had your chance, but you threw me over for that redhead."

He was obviously referring to the first night that Wyatt had tried to get him to go out on the town, but then Fiona had showed up in a fury. And turned his world upside down. Just like a monster fire…

"I might give you a second chance, though," Braden joked, "if you ask nicely."

"You just want to go out with me again," Wyatt said, "because women wind up tearing off your clothes."

Braden laughed. "I'm surprised you'd admit they'd rather see me naked than you."

If not for Fiona, he would have challenged him— would have initiated some silly game, like who could get the most phone numbers at a bar. He and Cody had played games like that—games that meant nothing to them because no woman ever really had.

Fiona had changed that. She had changed him. That was what women like her did. If anyone had ever been able to get him to quit the team, it would have been her. That was why he had to stay away.

"Maybe I should head out West," Wyatt said. He switched from the bag to the weight bench.

"For women?"

"For the season," he said. "You know that's where something's bound to start—if it hasn't already. Then instead of getting flown out, I'd already be there."

"Wyatt, that's not a good idea."

"Other members of the team are already out there." Already waiting for the season while working at other forestry stations across the country.

"Exactly," Braden said. "That's why I need you here. That's why it's better we're stationed centrally. We'll be ready no matter where it starts."

He hadn't been ready—not for Fiona. He'd thought he could handle her, that he could keep it to just sex between them. He'd thought himself incapable of falling for a woman like her. He had been such a fool. Every bit the cocky idiot she'd always thought him.

"You're right," he agreed.

Braden sighed. "Ordinarily, I'd love to hear that, but I've got a sick feeling instead. I sent Cody out to check all the campsites."

He had been checking the sites, too. "Not many campers yet." It was still too cold.

"Some Boy Scout troops are camping this weekend," Braden said. "Going for some badge for sleeping outside even though it drops to freezing at night."

Wyatt had done that. With the right equipment, people could camp year-round.

"I'm going to check in with him," Braden said. "Then I'm going to come back and drag you out. Maybe we will go back to that club…"

"You actually want women fighting over you again?"

"Hey, it wasn't all bad," he murmured as he walked off.

The captain was doing better—albeit at Wyatt's expense. But that pleased him. If Braden could recover from his heartbreak, Wyatt would be fine. It wasn't as if he and Fiona had been married. They hadn't even really dated.

Yeah, he was going to be fine. Any minute now…

But that tight knot of tension remained low in his stomach while the pressure remained on his heart. When he and Braden went out later, he'd work on him—convince him to let him join some of the other team members in the West. That would be better. Getting away from Fiona…

Away from temptation.

He focused on the weight bar. While he waited for Braden to return, he would do some reps. The muscles in his arms were already burning, but he didn't care. He welcomed the physical pain. It was the emotional pain he needed to avoid.

Grunting as he was with each rep, he didn't hear the footsteps at first—not until they neared the weight bench. "What did Cody say?" he asked. "I'm sure he'd be happy to help you get your clothes torn off."

"Passing me off on your friend?" a female voice, sharp with anger, asked. "Is that how your team operates?"

His palms suddenly sweaty, he nearly dropped the

bar. He quickly settled it into the holders and slid from beneath it. "I was talking to Braden again," he said.

She glanced around the gym, which was empty but for the two of them. "I don't see anyone else here."

"I didn't know you were, either," he pointed out. "Why are you here? And why are you so damn angry?"

Sure, he'd left in a rush—with little explanation for his strange panic. But she'd done that to him, too, the first time they'd had sex. She'd snuck out while he'd slept. At least she'd been awake…

She thrust a crumpled paper in his face. "You knew it—you already knew he'd been rejected!"

"Oh…"

Matt's letter had finally come. He'd thought they'd been mailed out weeks ago.

"You're not going to deny it?"

"I don't lie," he said.

She snorted. "Why do men never realize that a lie of omission is still a lie?"

"Don't compare me to that weaselly accountant," he said, and anger coursed through him now. "I would have told you if I was dating other women. And I would have told you about Matt…"

"But you'd wanted to sleep with me instead and you knew I wouldn't have had anything to do with you if not for my brother."

Anger snapped his control and he jerked her body against his. His hand on the back of her head, he held her still. And then he kissed her—hungrily and passionately. He kissed her until she kissed him back with just as much hunger and passion. Then he pulled away, and between gasps for breath, he asked, "Who's the liar now?"

Her heart beating so hard that he could see it in the rapid rise and fall of her breasts, she swung her hand and slapped him across the face.

His skin stung, and he blinked, lifting his hand to where he imagined the imprint of hers probably remained. His face was hot. But then he was hot all over—with desire for her. He reached for her again. He'd take her right there, in the firehouse gym. Standing up or on the weight bench. He didn't care where; he just had to have her—had to ease the unbearable tension in his body.

His hands had just closed around her shoulders when the alarm sounded, the siren piercing the air. "Damn…"

He had thought he wanted the fire; that he needed the distraction. But it was Fiona he wanted, Fiona he needed. "I would have told you," he said, "if I could have. But I'm not involved in the hiring process. I didn't know for sure…"

"You knew," she said.

He nodded. "I was pretty sure he wouldn't make it…"

He had that eerie feeling again—that ominous sensation burning in between his shoulder blades and low in his gut. "Fiona…"

But she'd already turned and was walking toward the doorway. Maybe because of the blaring alarm she didn't hear him. Or maybe she didn't care.

He would have run after her—would have chased her down and tried to explain his actions, or inactions, as it were. But the fire was here. He instinctively knew this was no small car fire on the side of the road. This was it—the monster Braden had been predicting for weeks.

Despite the slap, Wyatt was glad he'd kissed her—because that eerie sensation warned him it might be the last chance he'd had to do so, and not just because she was furious with him.

17

"YOU WERE RIGHT," Tammy said as she stared at the television over the bar in the curiously quiet Filling Station. Flames shimmered across the screen, smoke rising from the early spring vegetation the fire consumed.

The bar was probably quiet because the firefighters dedicated to the local firehouse were gone. Even the area volunteers had been called out since the fire was close. It roared through the national forest that surrounded the town.

The TV reporter assured the viewers that the town was in no danger. "This forest consists of several hundred acres. The Hotshot team has already set up breaks to stop the fire from jumping toward the town. They are working now on making a break around the area of campsites on the other side of the fire."

"Who'd be camping now?" Tammy murmured with a shiver of cold and distaste. Her friend was no camper.

"What was I right about?" Fiona asked.

Tammy gestured toward the television screen. "Firefighters are too great a risk. Good thing I didn't go for it with hunky Dawson Hess."

Fiona wondered now about her friend. While she met a lot of men, she didn't often do much beyond flirting with them. Usually she blamed the man—like saying the stripping police officer was impotent. "Why didn't you?"

Tammy shrugged. "Guess we've been friends so long that I've started thinking like you." She glanced up at the TV screen and all those flames and shuddered. "You're making me—" she paused, obviously for dramatic effect, before continuing with a sarcastic flourish *"—cautious."*

Fiona managed a smile. "You say that like it's a bad thing."

Tammy bumped her shoulder against Fiona's. "I will deny it if you say this to anyone else…" She glanced around the nearly empty bar as if someone might overhear them. "I think it's actually a good thing. Being cautious saved you from a lot of heartache with that sexy Wyatt Andrews."

Fiona blinked against the tears blurring her vision. And she couldn't take her attention from the fire; she had to see what was happening, had to know if Wyatt was all right.

"Oh, damn," Tammy murmured. "It's too late for you, isn't it?"

Fiona nodded. It was too late. Even though she was furious with him, she still loved Wyatt. And the last thing she'd done was slap him for kissing her. What if that had been their last kiss?

"Here you are," a male voice murmured.

Had he been sent back? Was he safe?

But when she spun around, it was Matthew she saw through her tears. His face was tense with worry—for her. He reached for her, but she swiveled the stool back toward the TV. She had to keep watching the blaze. The fire was consuming acres of forest and everything within that forest, as well. Somewhere in there was Wyatt.

"Sis," Matthew said. "Are you okay?"

No. She was a mess, her heart racing—her breathing fast and shallow. She was on the verge of a panic attack.

"Where is he?" she asked, peering at the TV as if she might see him within the flames. "Will he be okay?"

"Of course he will," Matthew assured her. "He's Wyatt. He knows what he's doing. He'll be just fine." While she appreciated his effort to comfort her, she heard the hollow ring of her brother's words. He didn't believe what he was saying any more than she did.

Wyatt was in a lot of danger. Despite all of his expertise, there was no guarantee that he would make it out alive.

IT WAS TURNING on him—just as Fiona had. And it was even hotter and angrier than she'd been either time she had stomped into the firehouse workout room.

The fire felt like a living entity. But he had to keep going. His shoulders burned as he held the chainsaw, cutting through tree after tree. He was trying to knock down some of the fuel—trying to build the break between the fire and the campsite. He couldn't hear the hum of the chainsaws wielded by his team members. Maybe because the crackle of the fire had grown louder; maybe because he'd become separated from them. He was moving faster, urgency coursing through him. He had to find those kids—the Boy Scouts trying to earn their early camping badges—before the fire consumed them as it had all the trees and new grass.

No one had heard from the Scout leaders. The campers were lost. And the Hotshots had to find them before they were lost forever.

Wyatt was a sawyer—one of the guys who cut down the fuel. Swampers followed them and would clean up the fuel so they could build the break. But the wind was picking up, shifting.

He could see sparks riding on the air—dancing in a different direction than they had earlier. Beneath his helmet his radio crackled as someone hit their switch to speak. Maybe a Scout leader had contacted someone at the command center.

"Wyatt, where are you?" Braden asked through the headset. He was no longer the captain of their small-town firehouse. He was the superintendent of the twenty-member Hotshot crew.

Wyatt cut power to his chainsaw and reached for the talk button on his radio. "I'm where you told me to be," he replied. As an assistant superintendent, he'd taken over for Braden when he'd returned to the command center to assess the fire and discuss strategy with the other fire teams. "I'm leading the sawyers cutting the break."

"Dawson said they lost sight of you…"

Hess was the other assistant superintendent; every Hotshot team had two. He was leading up the swampers today.

"They'd be a ways behind me," Wyatt pointed out. But he turned back to look. He saw only smoke.

The radio crackled again. "Wyatt?" It was Cody's voice now. "Where the hell are you?"

"In the lead," he said. Too far in the lead. He'd gotten separated from the other members of his team.

"I can't see you anymore, man," Cody said.

The younger man was fast; he shouldn't have been that far behind Wyatt. But the smoke was thickening—becoming almost impenetrable. Maybe he wasn't that far behind him.

"This thing is shifting." Braden said what Wyatt had already realized. "I'm pulling the team out. Now!"

"Those kids are out here," Wyatt said. "They don't have the right equipment to survive the fire." Not even Boy Scouts were prepared for a monster like this.

"It's too dangerous," Braden said. "I can't risk the entire team on what might prove to be a suicide mission."

"Then don't," Wyatt said. "Pull the rest of them."

"Wyatt!"

"I'm already separated from them." Caught between his team and those hapless campers.

"We'll find you," Cody said. "You can't be that far ahead of us. You're old and slow."

Wyatt chuckled—like the younger man had wanted him to. He was older than Cody but only by a few years. "And yet you can't keep up with me," he teased the other man. "So who's the slow one?"

"Since you're so fast," Braden cut in, "get your asses back here. Now!"

Wyatt scanned the area again. The radio had gone curiously quiet, so he listened for the sound of chainsaws. He doubted that Cody would have stopped yet. But he heard only the crackle and roar of the fire.

It was close. Too close.

He could turn back the way he'd come—follow the

break back to his crew. But that was away from the campers. Could he leave them out there alone? Especially now that the fire had shifted.

He remembered being that eleven-year-old kid watching the news—knowing that his parents were vacationing somewhere in the midst of the wildfire that had monopolized all the television broadcasts. He'd been scared for them.

Those kids out at the campsite were the age he'd been, and they were out there watching the fire come toward them. They were scared for themselves. And somewhere, their parents watched the news, terrified for their children.

He couldn't turn back. He couldn't save himself without first trying to save those kids. He owed it to them—and he owed it to that Hotshot who'd broken away from his crew, who'd given his life trying to save Wyatt's parents.

So that man hadn't died in vain, Wyatt had to try to rescue those kids. He turned away from the direction of his team and instead turned toward the campsite area—just as the fire had.

He knew what he had to do, and he had only one regret. Fiona...

Was she watching the news like those parents were? Was she worried about him? Or was she so mad that she didn't care what happened to him?

He was glad that he'd kissed her—even though he could still feel the imprint of her hand against his face. Hell, he was glad of that, too.

Maybe it was better that she'd been angry with him at the end. Because he worried that it wasn't just their relationship that had ended, but maybe his life, too.

18

"How did you get us in here?" Fiona whispered in wonder as she looked around the tent that had been set up at the edge of the safe zone—just outside Northern Lakes. From here Superintendent Braden Zimmer commanded his team of Hotshots.

Matthew shook his head. "I didn't get us in here. You did."

"I did?"

"Everybody knows you're Wyatt's girlfriend."

But that wasn't true. She and Wyatt hadn't actually been seeing each other. They'd only been using each other. "I'm not…"

Braden was the only one of Wyatt's friends that she recognized. The others had to be out at the fire still—with him. She wanted to talk to the superintendent. But he was busy, talking into a radio and with other fire crew leaders who stood around him.

What was going on? She could sense the urgency in Braden and see the tension in his face. Something was wrong.

Or maybe that was how he acted at every fire. Leading a crew of Hotshots had to be a stressful job. He was sending them out into the blaze—risking their lives. She couldn't imagine his level of responsibility or anxiety.

Just watching him made her fearful. Had he seen her? Was that how she and Matthew had been allowed inside the tent? Maybe he'd gestured to someone that it was okay to let them in. But why hadn't he come over to her?

Why wouldn't he even look at her now?

Sure, he was busy. But she worried that it was something more. Something far, far worse…

"I'm sorry," Matthew said.

And she jumped, fear overwhelming her. "What are you sorry about?"

Had he heard something? She could barely hear over the sound of her own pulse pounding in her ears. Other people spoke—inside the tent. And outside, where the reporters had been stopped at the perimeter. But she couldn't hear their individual voices—just the dull din of them all combined. She wished she could hear Superintendent Zimmer. But he was too far away and too focused on whatever he was saying into the radio.

If only she could read lips…

Maybe Matthew could.

"Why are you sorry?" she asked again—anxiously. And she focused on him instead of all the people around them.

But he looked away from her. His shoulders slumped with guilt and regret, he said, "I shouldn't have blamed you because the forest service rejected me as a candidate for the forestry fire department."

Guilt flashed through her now. She didn't deserve

his apology when she'd had every intention of doing whatever was necessary to prevent him from joining. It didn't matter that she actually hadn't had to do anything at all.

If she believed him, Wyatt hadn't done anything, either. He'd had nothing to do with the hiring process—just as he'd told her all along. And she believed him.

He didn't lie. Maybe he wasn't always as forthcoming with what he knew as she would like. But he didn't lie.

Neither would she.

"I would have stopped you," she told her brother. "If I could have…" Especially now as she stared at all the worried faces around them. She wasn't the only one concerned for a loved one. There were so many others. Wives and families of the other Hotshots?

Many of the women looked like *women like her*. Women who would have a hard time handling their husband or significant other risking his life every day he did his job.

Matthew sighed. "Wyatt must have never intended to recommend me for a position on the Hotshot team anyway."

"What position?" someone asked. She and Matthew turned toward the young man who'd approached them. The kid had curly dark hair and big brown eyes full of curiosity.

"Isn't there a position opening up on the team?" Matthew asked the question. Fiona couldn't have cared less; she cared only about finding out if Wyatt was okay.

If he was safe…

If he would be getting out of the fire soon…

The young man shook his head. "No, Cody Malle-han took the last one a year or so ago. There aren't any current openings, and knowing how well this team works together, there won't be any in the near future, either."

Matthew's jaw dropped open in shock. Maybe Fiona was getting hysterical, because a laugh slipped between her lips at his reaction.

"All of this and there wasn't even an opening?" Or maybe he'd thought he could get on the team just because he wanted to. Then she laughed again because she'd thought the same thing.

She had been such a fool. She understood now why Wyatt had kept assuring her she had nothing to worry about. Without revealing too much, he'd been trying to let her know that there was no danger of Matthew making the team. Because there was no opening...

Even if the forest service had hired him as a fire-fighter, he wouldn't have been able to join a Hotshot team for maybe years. Not that she wanted him to be a firefighter, either. That was nearly as dangerous as being a Hotshot.

"We're a couple of idiots," she told her brother.

He grimaced, his face a study in misery. He had re-ally wanted this—so much that he had quit school. He hadn't wanted the backup plan she'd suggested; he'd wanted only this.

Sympathy warmed her heart for him, and she squeezed his arm. "I'm sorry," she said.

"For calling me an idiot?" he asked, his lips curved into a faint, strained smile.

She shook her head. "For the rejection. I know you

really wanted this." She squeezed his arm again. "I'm sorry…"

He flinched as if her apology was a slap in the face. But he didn't pull away from her. Instead, he wrapped an arm around her shoulder and gave her a half hug. It was more than she'd gotten out of him in years.

She blinked away the tears stinging her eyes and, as Wyatt always had, she teased. "Don't worry. I'm the bigger idiot because I actually fell for Wyatt." And the tears rushed back, choking her voice and filling her vision.

His other arm slid around her, and he pulled her fully into a hug. "I'm sorry, sis…"

She nodded, but she couldn't speak. Not yet…

"I shouldn't have brought you here," Matthew said. "It'll be too hard on you."

She pulled back, her body tense. Too hard on her? Did he suspect she would hear only bad news here? Did he doubt Wyatt would make it out alive?

Because she was beginning to have those doubts herself…

"We can leave," Matthew suggested. "We don't have to stay here."

But then a ripple went through the crowd—a gasp of horror. A silence followed it—broken only when someone asked, "Is it true?"

"What?" a man standing beside Superintendent Zimmer asked. He wore firefighting gear, too, but his wasn't the bright yellow Braden and his team wore. But it was only Braden and this man in black and gray who actually looked like firefighters inside the tent.

The rest of the firefighters were out battling the fire. But those on the front lines were the Hotshots; they were the soldiers who stormed the beach. But maybe it was easier to dodge bullets than flames.

"A reporter outside just claimed that the fire shifted," an older man said.

That was the ripple that had gone through the crowd, each person repeating the news to the next like the childhood game of telephone.

Braden stepped up to a podium at the front of the tent. His face tense and eyes dark, he confirmed, "The fire has shifted."

"What does that mean?" Someone asked the question on Fiona's lips. The woman was like her, her face white with fear. Tears streamed from her haunted eyes. "Is it heading toward the campsite?"

Braden hesitated for just a moment before nodding. "Unfortunately, yes."

That woman screamed; another shrieked in terror.

And Fiona began to shake.

A man cleared his throat and asked, "What does this mean? Is there no hope for our kids?"

"Kids?" Fiona whispered.

And Matthew's face paled, too. His arm tightened around her. But she wasn't sure if he was offering her comfort or seeking it.

The curly-haired young man standing near them spoke again, softly, "A Boy Scout troop was camping in the middle of the national forest. The Hotshots were trying to cut a break between the campsite and the fire, to keep it away from them and get them out…"

The other man—in the gray and black—stepped up to the podium with Braden. "I'm the spokesperson for this information post," he said. "Captain Cowell."

The dad, who'd just spoken, spoke again, "We've gotten very little information so far."

Apparently Braden agreed, because he shouldered aside the spokesperson and reached for the microphone. "I've been in contact with my team of Hotshots on the front line of the fire. They're not just setting up the break. They're doing a search and rescue, too."

Someone sighed with relief.

But the others, like Fiona, saw the tension on the superintendent's face.

"Something's happened," the dad said.

"The fire shifted," Braden repeated what he'd said the first time he'd stepped to the mike.

"What does that mean?"

This time it was a different question. It wasn't a request for a definition of a term but for more information.

Braden recognized it for what it was. "I had to call my team out," he said.

"Why!" A woman shrieked the question.

Despite how Braden had taken over, the official spokesperson jumped to his defense. "He couldn't risk the lives of all of his men. Some of them have families, too. Children of their own…"

It had been a tough call. Fiona could see that on Braden's face. But he'd called out the team. They were coming back. They would be safe.

"What about our kids?" the dad asked again, his voice cracking with fear. Other parents held each other and sobbed.

Guilt and sympathy both filled Fiona. She clutched at her brother as the feelings overwhelmed her. She was grateful that Wyatt would be safe, but at what cost to these families?

Braden leaned toward the mike again. "One of my men refused to leave," he said. "He refused to come back without at least trying to perform a rescue." And finally he looked at Fiona, his gaze meeting hers across that crowded tent.

She knew which man had been insubordinate, which one would have willingly disregarded his own safety to save the lives of others.

"Has he found them?" the dad asked.

Braden shook his head. Then he cleared his throat and added, "We lost radio contact with him some time ago."

A gasp rippled through the crowd. This time it emanated from Fiona. The pain stabbing her heart confirmed her greatest fear. Wyatt…

He was lost.

Braden met her gaze again and held it, speaking only to her in that tent full of people. "A couple other members of the team insisted on going back for him."

Translation: they had been insubordinate, too. From the way they'd jumped to his defense during that bar fight, she could guess who: Dawson Hess and Cody Mallehan.

"They'll find him and the kids…" Braden sounded as though he was just trying to convince himself now— that he hadn't lost three men.

"Maybe there will be an opening after all," that young man murmured before moving through the crowd.

Fiona shivered. And Matthew slid his arm around her, offering her comfort. "The kid's wrong," he assured her. "Wyatt will make it out."

Wyatt had been Matthew's hero for years and was therefore invincible in his eyes. Fiona knew that he was actually just a man—a man who had willingly put his life on the line to rescue others. She should have been furious with him for taking that risk. She should have been furious with herself for falling for him even though she'd known he routinely took such risks.

But as she watched all those distraught parents, all she could do was thank God for men like Wyatt Andrews—brave men full of heart and determination who knew no fear.

WYATT HAD NEVER been so afraid. His heart raced with it as his lungs struggled for breath. He'd had to don his oxygen mask. But was there enough? Would it last?

Did it matter? He wasn't sure how the hell he was going to make it out of the fire. But that was the least of his concerns. They were his concern. He stepped from the smoke into the middle of a nightmare.

The twelve kids looked like statues—huddled together—as if that would protect them. The Scout leaders, two young men who didn't look much older than the kids of whom they were in charge, stood over them. He could see them shaking with fear, with indecision.

They had strayed from the campsite. That was why it had been harder to find them. But even through the smoke, he'd found their tracks—the footprints, the broken branches. They'd run from the fire as hard and fast as they could. But that was before it had shifted. Soon it would overcome them.

Knowing that they were going after campers, Wyatt had grabbed a couple extra packs. But he didn't have enough shelters—the aluminized sleeping bags—for everyone.

He removed his oxygen mask and spoke loudly, to be heard over the crackling fire. "We need to move."

If he could get them to land that the fire had already consumed, they might have a chance. He clapped his gloves together, but they made no sound. The gesture snapped the kids out of their paralysis, though, and they began to move. But the fire was too close. There wasn't enough time to get them back to burned land.

He looked for the next best thing—for bare land. It had been a rough winter in northeastern Michigan— rough enough that not all the vegetation had started growing back yet. He found an area that might work. He dropped his packs and pulled out some picks and small shovels. "Help me clear," he told them. If they could get the land bare…

The kids were small, though. And scared. And the Scout leaders were equally as terrified. He needed more help or none of them would make it when the fire caught them.

And it would…

HOURS LATER, WYATT led the ragged troop out of the still-smoldering forest. He couldn't believe they'd made it back. He actually wasn't certain they had…until he saw her.

Of course, she could be an angel, because if angels existed, they couldn't be any more beautiful than she was. She moved around the staging tent, bringing cups of coffee and bottles of water to nervous couples who sat around, clutching each other. She offered comforting pats on shoulders, squeezed hands. And all the while her face remained tight with her own worry and fear.

She was afraid for him? Even after how he'd misled her, she cared about him. Sure, he hadn't been able to tell her anything about Matt's application. But he could have more heartily assured her the kid had no chance of making the team. He had not been as honest with her as he should have been. He didn't deserve her.

And she didn't deserve to feel that fear. She'd told him why she hadn't wanted to get involved with him. She'd told him that she couldn't fall for a man like him—one who risked his life. She'd said she wouldn't survive the worry and the eventual loss. But he had put her through it anyway.

He had to let her go. He'd thought it before, that they were over. That this—whatever it was—was truly done.

When he'd been out in that fire—in the thick of the smoke and the heat of the flames—he had admitted to himself what it really was. Love.

He loved Fiona O'Brien. And because he loved her, he'd fought the fire. He'd battled through the blaze to get back to her.

Only to let her go.

Because there would be other fires, and he wouldn't be able to fight them without thinking of her, looking so terrified as she rushed around the tent. He never wanted her to experience that fear again.

Finally the crowd turned and noticed them standing there—him, Cody and Dawson and the little kids with their soot-streaked faces. Their eyes wide with fear and exhaustion.

First an eerie silence fell over the tent. Then shrieks of joy rang out.

19

Fiona's heart lifted with hope as the parents vaulted out of their seats and rushed toward their children. The kids had survived the fire. Had Wyatt?

Then she saw him, standing tall behind them. His face black with soot, his hair slick with sweat. He had never looked more handsome to her. He was staring at her, his blue eyes wide, as if he couldn't believe she was there.

She was the one who'd thought she would never see him again. Before she could get to him, people surrounded him. Parents thumped his back and hugged him, pouring out gratitude for what he had done.

For saving their kids...

If not for Wyatt and men like him, how many lives would be lost every year?

"You get it now?" Matthew asked her.

Emotion choking her, she could only nod. She got it. She understood that she had misjudged her brother. Maybe he hadn't wanted the job for the thrill of danger and the glory of being the hero or even for the women. Maybe he'd only wanted to save people like Wyatt had.

"I'm sorry," she told her brother. "I'm sorry you didn't make the department."

"It wasn't your fault," he said.

"But I know you wanted it," she said. "And now I understand why. You can always apply again."

His eyes widened with shock at her encouragement. And she realized how right Wyatt had been in how he'd handled her brother and how he'd advised her to handle him. He'd offered support and encouragement.

All she had done was criticize his choices.

"Thanks," he said. "But I think I'll go back to school. I'll finish up my degree." He smiled and waited. "What? No whoop of victory?"

She shook her head. "I don't want to win," she said. "I just want you to be happy." And that was all she ever should have wanted for him. He was a grown man—not the little boy she'd been forced to leave. She couldn't protect him from pain or from the dangers of the world. All she could do was love him.

"I want the same for you, sis," he said. And he followed her gaze to Wyatt.

Most of all, she had misjudged Wyatt.

She knew now why he did what he did—so nobody else would suffer the way he had when he'd lost his parents in that fire all those years ago. He had been about the age these boys were; maybe it was that sense of kinship with them that had compelled him to ignore Braden's orders. Or maybe just sheer stubbornness…

Either way, he had done the right thing. He'd saved lives. Camera bulbs flashed as reporters took photos from their positions just outside the tent. His handsome, soot-streaked face would probably be on the front of every local paper, maybe even some national magazines.

He was a hero. Not just to the families of the Boy Scouts. Or even to the nation. He was her hero, too.

HAD SHE LEFT? Wyatt wouldn't blame her if she had. This wasn't the life she'd wanted. It was the exact opposite of the safe, stable world she had created for herself. That she needed…

He needed her—so much he almost considered giving up the job. At least, the thought had passed through his mind when he'd worried that he wouldn't get those scared kids to safety. If he'd failed to rescue them and had risked never seeing Fiona again, never kissing her, never tasting her…

What would have been the point of being a Hotshot?

But now, seeing the joy on the faces of the kids' families, Wyatt wasn't sure he could walk away.

Even for her…

A strong hand gripped his arm, pulling him around. He expected the embrace of another grateful father. He'd been hugged so many times he'd lost count. But it was Braden instead—pulling him into a tight embrace. Their Huron Hotshots team was close, as a rule, but they didn't usually openly display emotion.

They'd be more likely to slug each other than hug each other, and after Wyatt had ignored his direct order, Braden had every reason to hit him. Especially when he should have known his insubordination would lead others to disobey orders, as well. After Cody and Dawson had gotten the rest of the team out, they'd come back for him—just in time. They'd helped him and the kids clear the land down to bare dirt. Then they'd had to squeeze themselves, the kids and Scout leaders into the special shelters. Fortunately, Dawson had thought to bring extra packs with him, as well.

For once putting all his joking aside, Wyatt told his superintendent, "I'm sorry."

"You made the right call," Braden admitted. "You saved fourteen lives."

"I didn't do it alone." He shifted, trying to ease out of his boss's hug.

But then he realized the reason the superintendent had wanted to get so close when Braden whispered, "Looks like arson…"

Son of a bitch…

Anger coursed through him. Someone had purposely set that fire—had purposely destroyed acres of land and nearly the lives of a dozen kids. He cursed aloud. But Braden finally pulled back and shook his head.

The last thing they needed was for this to leak to the media before they'd had a chance to investigate fully. He nodded in understanding.

"You kept saying this one was going to be a monster," Cody said as he joined them. "I'm never going to doubt you again."

Braden slapped Cody, lightly, upside the head. "Be certain that you don't," he admonished the newest member of the team. While he hadn't scolded Wyatt or even accepted his apology, Braden needed to remind Cody who was in charge.

He was young, more in maturity than years. But he would learn—if he stuck around. Growing up a foster kid, Cody was used to moving around a lot. That was why being a Hotshot had appealed to him. But being on the team was like having a family. Cody had never had that before. Wyatt wondered if it would be enough to make Cody want to stay.

Braden and Cody walked away to join Dawson. They spoke in hushed tones. Anyone else would have probably considered it a debriefing or maybe even a dressing down, but Wyatt knew Braden was telling them about the arson.

He needed to join them. Ordinarily they wouldn't investigate an arson. They wouldn't do anything but put out the heart of the fire. But this was different.

It had happened in their home base. In their national forest.

It was personal.

Before Wyatt could move, another hand slapped his back—like so many hands had before. He wasn't sure he deserved the praise; maybe he would have learned more from the slap Braden had given Cody. He needed some sense knocked into him. How had he considered—even for a moment—giving up the job? Especially when there was somebody out there deliberately setting fires.

This one might not have been his first. But Wyatt knew for certain that it wouldn't be the arsonist's last. Firebugs didn't stop starting fires until they were caught. And sometimes, even then, they couldn't help themselves…

The back slapper murmured, "I'm glad you made it safely out…"

He turned to Matt, and his heart twisted with regret. The poor kid had been so disappointed—in Wyatt, in his sister. "I'm surprised you came down," he said. During their last confrontation, Matt had disowned him as both a friend and a mentor.

"Of course I came down," Matt said. "You've been there for me the past six years. I wanted to be here for you."

Apparently they were friends again. Wyatt was glad.

"So did she," Matt said. "I brought Fiona."

Remembering how he'd seen her when he'd first stepped into the tent, so tense and terrified, Wyatt shook his head. "That might not have been a good idea."

"It actually was." Matt beamed with pride. "She was great. She *is* great."

For those few moments when they'd first appeared unannounced, Wyatt had watched her. He'd seen how, even as scared as she'd been, she had tried to take care of and comfort everyone. She was amazing.

"Yes, she is."

"I was wrong about her," Matt said. "I was wrong about so many things…"

He was glad that the kid had finally come to his senses and gained an appreciation for his sister. "You should take her home," Wyatt suggested. "She must be exhausted."

"I'm not going anywhere," a soft voice remarked. There was steel beneath the softness—a strength he'd known existed but the depth of which he hadn't guessed.

"You should know by now not to argue with her," Matt said. He pulled Wyatt into a tight hug and murmured, "I'm sorry."

Before Wyatt could ask him why, the kid slipped away through the crowd—leaving Fiona with him. "Why'd he apologize?"

"Either because he knows you had nothing to do with his not getting hired into the fire department," she said, "or because he left me here with you." Her brow furrowed as she stared after her brother, and she said, "I'm sorry that he did."

He was the one who owed her the apology. For so many things...

"You're busy here." She glanced outside the tent at the all-pervasive smoke. "The fire might not even be out yet. Do you have to go back?"

He listened for the fear he was certain the thought inspired in her. But he heard nothing in her voice. Maybe she didn't care as much as he'd thought.

"We got the breaks in," he said. "It's contained now and should be out soon."

She uttered a sigh of relief. "That's good. That's great."

"I don't have to go back out," he said. This time. But there would be other fires. Would she be able to handle that? Would she want to?

"I have other stuff I need to do, though..." Like help catch an arsonist. "I'll have to have someone drive you home."

"No."

The sharpness of her tone startled him. "Fiona, are you all right?"

She shook her head as if she wasn't. But then she murmured, "I'm so happy..." even as tears filled her eyes.

A twinge of pain struck his heart—with regret and guilt. He hated that he had made her cry. He had to let her go; he couldn't put her through this again.

But then she was hugging him, her arms winding tightly around his back. Even through his gear, he could feel the soft crush of her breasts. Maybe he could even feel the heat of her body—or perhaps it was just the vividness of his imagination and his memories of their bodies being so close, sliding over each other.

He had to smell like smoke and sweat and sawdust. But she buried her face in his chest as if she didn't care. Of course, she smelled like smoke, too. It was so thick in the air that it had permeated everything. He needed a shower. But most of all he needed her.

Could he find the selflessness to push her away? He moved his hands to her shoulders. But he couldn't bring himself to shove her back. He couldn't bring himself to do anything but close his arms around her and hold on to her.

He flinched as cameras flashed again—reporters finding a photo op in their embrace. Maybe they thought she was another grateful parent. If they asked what she was to him, he wasn't sure what he would say.

He might only be able to admit the truth to himself— that she was the love of his life.

20

FIONA FLOATED ON a wave of love, buoyed by her feelings for Wyatt and her relief that he was alive. Was he actually alive? Or had she dreamed it? Had she just imagined him walking into that tent with all those kids he'd rescued?

For just a second, she let herself imagine the alternative—that he hadn't come out of the fire. That the flames had consumed him...

She jerked awake with a scream on her lips and the smell of smoke burning her nostrils.

"Shh..." a deep voice murmured. "I've got you." Strong arms tightened around her as he carried her upstairs. His boots clomped heavily against the cement steps while cement block walls lined the stairwell. "You're okay..."

More important, he was okay. He was alive.

A sigh of relief slipped through her lips. Then she ran her fingers through his hair and clung to him. He was warm and strong and real. She wasn't dreaming. But she glanced around, uncertain of their location.

"Where are we?" she asked.

She'd gone back with him to the firehouse for his debriefing. Before waking up in Wyatt's arms, the last thing she remembered was lying down on the couch in Superintendent Zimmer's office.

"We're still at the firehouse," he said. "I need to shower."

A smile curved her lips. "Why are you carrying me?"

He sniffed at her hair. "Because you need to shower, too."

She gasped at the salacious thought, but then quickly returned to reality. "What about the other members of your team?"

"They can shower alone," he said.

"Wyatt!"

"They actually already did. They're all gone," he assured her. "It's just you and me." His footsteps echoed hollowly as he left the stairwell and started down a hall. The building certainly sounded empty.

"They went home?" she asked.

He nodded. "The fire's contained. It's burning itself out. It won't be much longer now."

She breathed a sigh of relief. The fire had burned for hours before Matthew had brought her to the command center. And they'd spent hours there, waiting for word on Wyatt. Waiting to see if he made it out…

So the fire, the monster Superintendent Zimmer had predicted, had burned for a couple of days already. Now that it was contained, it would be out soon. She hoped.

"But there will be more fires," he warned her.

She knew it. Of course there would be. But he seemed a little more certain than that. Or maybe he was just trying to scare her away again.

He dropped his arm from beneath her legs so that her feet touched the floor. And he steadied her outside a door. "Here's the women's locker room."

"Are there women on your team?" she asked.

He nodded. "A couple."

"Are they gone, too?"

"Everyone's gone," he said.

"Then I'll shower with you…"

He groaned and closed his eyes, as if just the thought alone turned him on.

He turned her on. She wanted him. She needed him. She pressed her body against his and linked her arms around his neck. Pulling his head down for her kiss, she found his mouth with hers. And she kissed him deeply, pressing her lips to his.

He groaned again. But he pulled back. With a shuddery sigh, he leaned his forehead against hers and said, "Fiona, we need to talk…"

"You talk too much," she told him playfully, teasingly.

But he was all serious. No glint of humor in his blue eyes at all. Just redness from the smoke and exhaustion. The last thing he needed was talk now. But he persisted.

"You never let me talk enough," he said. "I tried to tell you that you didn't need to worry about Matt. I knew he wouldn't get on to the team."

She remembered a few times that he had tried to talk about it, and she'd stopped him. Because, like now, she wanted to make love with him instead. If she'd let him assure her that Matthew wouldn't make the team, she would have had no excuse to sleep with him—to fall for him.

She tentatively admitted, "You did try…"

He sighed. "I know. I should have tried harder," he said, as if she'd criticized his efforts. "I should have made it clearer…"

Guilt tugged at her, and she admitted, "I wasn't exactly honest with you, either. I was trying to seduce you into helping me talk Matthew out of becoming a firefighter."

He chuckled. "You're not exactly Mata Hari. I knew what you were up to. I should have done the honorable thing. But I wanted you too damn much…"

She understood because that want—that need— overwhelmed her. She had never felt such passion before, such desire. Over his shoulder she noticed the door for the men's locker room. She grasped his hand and tugged him across the hall and through that door.

"Fiona…"

"You smell like smoke," she reminded him. But he didn't just smell like it. Soot streaked his handsome face—darker even than the stubble on his jaw. She tugged up his T-shirt and found that the soot had penetrated his gear and his shirt to streak across his skin. She tossed the shirt aside and ran her palms over his chest and down the washboard muscles of his stomach. Her skin came away black, too.

"You're going to get dirty showering with me," he warned her as he kicked off his boots beside the locker emblazoned with his name. But he took her hand now and led her past the lockers to the stark white painted cement walls of the shower area. He turned on a faucet that had water flowing from all the showerheads.

She squealed as the not-yet-warmed water blasted her face and hair. It heated quickly, though—especially when Wyatt kicked off his jeans and boxers and stood before her gloriously naked and aroused.

She probably didn't look too desirable with her smoke-permeated hair hanging wetly around her face and her clothes soaked with water and soot. She hurriedly discarded them so, like him, she could feel the water sluicing over her bare skin.

But then it wasn't just water. His hands caressed her, sliding over her shoulders, down along her waist and hips. A gasp of desire escaped her lips. She wanted to touch him, too. But she soaped her hands first, then glided them over his skin, washing away the soot. The water turned black as it ran down their legs and across the white tile floor to the drains.

Even when, finally, the water ran clear, she didn't stop soaping his skin. She didn't stop caressing him. She ran her hands all over his body—his chest, his back, his butt, his stomach and lower...

Until she wrapped her fingers around him. She used both hands, gliding them up and down his shaft.

He groaned. And, lowering his head, he kissed her. Deeply. Passionately.

It wasn't enough. She wanted more than his kiss. She wanted all of him. He kept kissing her, but he touched her, too. His hands cupped her breasts, his thumbs stroking over her nipples.

She cried out as pleasure overwhelmed her. She'd been afraid that they were over—forever. That she would never be this close to him again. She wasn't close enough yet, though. She needed more. She kept stroking him. And she was apparently driving him as crazy as he was driving her because he pushed her back against the wall of the shower. While the floor was tile, the wall was concrete—cold and hard. But she barely noticed it. She was focused fully on him and the way he made her feel. So much…

He moved his hands from her breasts, skimming them around her hips and over her butt. He cupped her cheeks and lifted her against the wall. And as he lifted her, his fingers slid inside her.

She cried out again at the delicious sensation. But it wasn't enough. She wanted more. The pressure building inside her demanded more.

"Wyatt, please," she implored him, her fingertips stroking over the pulsing tip of his erection.

He groaned. Then he entered her fully in one thrust.

She moaned as he filled her. It wasn't enough. She wanted him deeper—wanted him to reach even farther inside. Despite the hardness of the wall at her back, she wriggled and arched, taking him as deep as she was able. She wrapped her legs around his waist and gripped his shoulders. And she rode him—sliding up and down his shaft.

She moaned again at the pleasure, at the sweet sensation of him moving within her. "You feel so good," she murmured. So perfect…

Muscles rippled in his shoulders and bulged in his arms. A cord stood out on the side of his neck as he struggled for control. "You're killing me, woman…"

But she was the one who screamed as pleasure shattered her, an orgasm shuddering through her. He didn't stop, though; he kept pulsing in and out, kept kissing her, exploring her mouth with his tongue as his cock thrust inside her. And as he kissed her, he teased her with his caresses. Then his fingers slid toward her clit. He stroked over it—back and forth. And she came again. This time she didn't just scream, she cried out, "I love you!"

He tensed. And first she thought she'd horrified him with her admission. But his hands gripped her hips. He thrust deep and came, filling her. He shouted at the release. But he made no admission of his own. Except for the sound of the water running, the room had gone eerily silent.

Her face heated with embarrassment and she wriggled free of his body. Her feet nearly slipped on the tiles. She grabbed a towel from a bench near the door to the locker room. But as she wrapped it around herself, she realized it was all she would have to wear. Her clothes lay soaked on the bathroom floor.

Then even the sound of water stopped as Wyatt turned off the faucet. His big hands cupped her shoulders, and he tried to spin her back toward him.

She resisted, but he was too strong. When she faced him, she closed her eyes, unwilling to see the pity in his gaze.

"I'm sorry," she said. "I know that's not what *this* is." Because she couldn't help herself, she reached out and moved her hands over his wet chest. "It's just sex…"

And that was all it would ever be to him.

"BULLSHIT," HE SAID—with so much force that she gasped and stared up at him in surprise. "It's not just sex, and you damn well know it."

Hope brightened her eyes. "I know what it is to me," she said. "But I don't know what it is to you…"

"Everything," he admitted. Wonderful. Overwhelming. Impossible. "It's *everything*. I love you, too." But he was stuck on the impossible, and the hopelessness and frustration made his voice gruff.

"Don't sound so happy about it," she said. And now her temper was back, flashing in her green eyes.

He loved his hot little redhead. Too much…

He loved her enough to let her go. "It's because I love you that I can't ask you to be with me."

She snorted. "I'm not looking for a marriage proposal."

"Not yet," he said. She was too cautious for that. But she was too cautious to be with him, as well. "But someday you would. And from now on, I'm going to be completely open and honest with you."

"You're not the marrying kind," she said. "I get that. You've made that abundantly clear."

"Do you know why?"

She shrugged, and her towel slipped down. Her breasts jiggled free, distracting him. And hardening him. He wanted her all over again.

She pulled the towel back up and tucked one end of it between her breasts. "Because you can't tie yourself to one woman."

"I can," he said, "if that woman's you."

Her lips parted on a soft gasp, and her eyes softened. He'd heard her love—when she'd shouted it as she came. Now he saw it—warming her eyes.

And his heart.

But he reminded himself that it was impossible, because it would never be fair to either of them.

"But I can't ask you to tie yourself to me." He closed his eyes as he remembered the expression on her face when he'd walked into that tent, that look of fear, before she'd seen him. "I can't put you through again what you went through today." He forced himself to release her—to step away.

He reached for a towel and, with shaking hands, wrapped it around his waist. "I know what I should do—that I should just give up the job."

"No!" She shouted the word with all the gravitas of an epitaph.

He tensed and turned back around, surprised at the vehemence of her tone. It was on her face, too—which was suddenly tense. He had thought she would instantly agree. "You matter more to me than it does."

She shook her head, and water spattered from the ends of her wet hair. She was so resolute and so beautiful. "It would kill you to give up the Hotshot team," she said. "And it would kill me if I caused you to give it up."

Water from her hair dripped down her shoulders. A bead of it trickled over the slope of her breast to disappear beneath the towel. He wanted to tug it off her. He wanted her. And not just again but *always*.

"Maybe I could do it," he said as he considered the idea. He would consider anything for her. "Maybe I could walk away…for you…with you…"

"You can't," she insisted. "You have to stay on the team. You're needed. All those families…" Her voice cracked with emotion. As he'd kept seeing that crippling fear on her face, she must have kept seeing it on theirs. She shuddered from the overwhelming emotion of it.

"Those parents needed you to save their kids," she said. "And you did. If something like that happened again…"

He had a horrible feeling that it would if they didn't catch the arsonist.

"And," she continued, "if you weren't there because of my fears, because of me…" She shook her head and shuddered again as the ramifications of that occurred to her.

"Those kids would have died," he admitted without arrogance. He'd been closer to the campsite than Cody and Dawson. He'd already gotten the campers farther from the fire when the others had found them.

"No." She uttered it again with such vehemence.

"What are you saying?"

"That I love you too much to ask you to give up what you love," she said.

His breath shuddered out with relief. But he still didn't know what it meant…for them. Could they have a future when they both wanted different things? Unfortunately he knew the answer.

"And I love you too much to ask you to live with your fears…" His relief left, sliding away like the water had down the drain—along with his hope. "You were right about what I do. It makes loving me too great a risk."

Especially for someone like her who knew all the mortality rates of every profession. His was more dangerous than most; today had proved that for her.

But she smiled. "You survived that fire," she said. "And you'll survive the next one and the one after that. There is no risk in loving you."

"You do love me," he murmured in awe of her sudden optimism and confidence. He'd known she was strong; she'd already proven her strength went deeper than he'd fathomed. But now he considered that it might be endless.

Her fears had nearly been realized; he could have died in that fire—that damn fire someone had set. But she loved him anyway.

She smiled, her face aglow, and told him just as vehemently as she'd told him no, "I am *so* in love with you…"

He reached for her towel, tugging it and her up against him. "And I am so in love with you."

He lowered his mouth to hers and kissed her with a tenderness that must have surprised her, because she gasped. His name escaped on a sigh between her parted lips.

He took advantage of her sigh to deepen the kiss. He moved his mouth over hers and then his tongue. She moaned and locked her arms around his neck.

Her towel dropped away. And he let his go, too. They were both naked again. She pressed against him, burrowing into his arms as if she couldn't get close enough.

His legs slightly shaky with exhaustion and awe in her love, he carried her only as far as the bench that held the towels. And he laid her down onto the softness of them. Then he covered her body with his. She lifted her legs, taking him deep as he entered her—joining them. They were as close as they could be, as if she were an extension of him—as much a part of him as his madly pounding heart. Their love and understanding and passion would bind them forever.

Tension gripped his body, almost making him shake before it broke. They came together—crying out simultaneously as ecstasy overwhelmed them. He had never felt so complete. Or so loved…

So fortunate.

He'd felt lucky when he'd made it out of that fire without losing a kid. But he hadn't known what good fortune was until now.

Fiona didn't just love him. She understood him— on a level no one else ever had. Wyatt had been wrong about her. So wrong. She wasn't one of those women— the ones who had used ultimatums to manipulate his former team members into quitting, into giving up what they loved. Maybe it hadn't been the women, though. Maybe his former teammates had made the decisions themselves—to not put their wives or families through what he'd put Fiona through today. He was so in love with her that he had been willing to give up the job for her. But she had refused. Fiona knew why he had become a Hotshot, and because she knew, she would never ask him to leave the team.

Instead she had become part of his team—the most important part to him. She was his heart and his incentive for surviving every fire. Because she would always be there when he came home.

* * * * *

REQUEST YOUR FREE BOOKS!
2 FREE NOVELS PLUS 2 FREE GIFTS!

⊞ HARLEQUIN®

Blaze®

red-hot reads!

HBI5

*Enjoy this sneak peek at A SEAL'S TOUCH
by* New York Times *bestselling
author* **Tawny Weber**—*a sexy, sizzling story in the*
UNIFORMLY HOT! *series from Harlequin Blaze!*

*Navy SEAL Taylor "The Wizard" Powell has a
reputation for getting out of tricky situations. Bad guys,
bombs—no problem. Finding a girlfriend in order to
evade matchmaking friends? Not so easy.*

Taylor Powell pulled his Harley into the driveway and cut
the engine.

Home.

He headed for the front door, located his key and
stepped inside.

"Yo," he called out as the door swung shut behind him.
"Ma?"

He heard a thump then a muffled bang.

"Ma?" His long legs ate up the stairs as he did a quick
mental review of his last CPR certification.

As he barreled past his childhood bedroom, he heard
another thump coming from the hall bathroom. This time
accompanied by cussing.

Very female, very unmotherly, cussing.

In a blink his tension dissipated.

He knew that cussing.

Grinning he sauntered down the hall. Stopping in the
bathroom door, he smiled in appreciation of the sweetly
curved rear end encased in worn denim.

The legs were about a mile long. The kind of legs that went beyond wrapping around a guy's waist.

He almost groaned when his eyes reached a pair of black leather boots similar to the ones he wore on duty. Was there anything sexier than legs like that in black boots?

"Hellooo," he murmured.

"What?" The hips moved, the back arched and the owner of those sexy legs lifted her head so fast he heard it hit something under the sink. Rubbing her head, the woman glared at him with enough heat to start a fire.

"Taylor?"

"Cat?" he said at the same time. He started to help her to her feet, but at the last second paused. Touching her so soon after that image of her legs wrapped around him didn't seem like a smart idea.

When the hell had Kitty Cat gotten hot?

Her golden hair was tied back, highlighting a face too strong to be called pretty. Eyes the color of the ocean at sunset stared back under sharply arched brows. The rounded cheeks and slight upper bite were familiar.

The way her faded green tee cupped her breasts was new, as was the sweetly gentle slide from breast to waist to hip where the tee met denim.

Oh, yeah. Kitty Cat was definitely hot.

"Hey there, Mr. Wizard," Cat greeted. "Still out saving the world?"

"As always. How about the Kitty Cat?"

"Same as ever," Cat said with a shrug that did interesting things to that T-shirt of hers.

Things he had no business noticing…

Don't miss A SEAL'S TOUCH by Tawny Weber, available February 2016!

Turn your love of reading into rewards you'll love with
Harlequin My Rewards

**Join for FREE today at
www.HarlequinMyRewards.com**

Earn **FREE BOOKS** of your choice.

Experience **EXCLUSIVE OFFERS** and contests.

Enjoy **BOOK RECOMMENDATIONS**
selected just for you.

PLUS! Sign up now
and get **500** points
right away!

Earn
FREE
REWARDS
Join
Today!
HarlequinMyRewards.com

MYR16R

HARLEQUIN®
A *Romance* FOR EVERY MOOD™

JUST CAN'T GET ENOUGH?

Join our social communities
and talk to us online.

You will have access to the latest
news on upcoming titles and special
promotions, but most importantly,
you can talk to other fans about your
favorite Harlequin reads.

Harlequin.com/Community

 Facebook.com/HarlequinBooks

 Twitter.com/HarlequinBooks

Pinterest.com/HarlequinBooks